GHOULISH SONG

Also by William Alexander

GOBLIN SECRETS

GHOULISH SONG

WILLIAM ALEXANDER

MARGARET K. McELDERRY BOOKS
New York London Toronto Sydney New Delhi

MARGARET K. McELDERRY BOOKS

An imprint of Simon & Schuster Children's Publishing Division

1230 Avenue of the Americas, New York, New York 10020

MARGARET K. McELDERRY BOOKS is a trademark of Simon & Schuster, Inc.

For information about special discounts for bulk purchases, please contact Simon & Schuster Special Sales at 1-866-506-1949 or business@simonandschuster.com.

The Simon & Schuster Speakers Bureau can bring authors to your live event. For more information or to book an event, contact the Simon & Schuster Speakers Bureau at 1-866-248-3049 or visit our website at www.simonspeakers.com.

The text for this book is set in Adobe Caslon.

Manufactured in the United States of America

0213 FFG

10 9 8 7 6 5 4 3 2 1

Library of Congress Cataloging-in-Publication Data

Alexander, William (William Joseph), 1976–

Ghoulish song / William Alexander. — 1st ed.

p. cm.

Summary: When the music of a bone flute given to her by a goblin separates Kaile's shadow from herself, her family believes she has died and become a ghoul, and Kaile must set out to prove that she still lives.

ISBN 978-1-4424-2729-7 — ISBN 978-1-4424-2731-0 (eBook)

[1. Fantasy. 2. Shadows—Fiction. 3. Music—Fiction. 4. Magic—Fiction. 5. Goblins—Fiction. 6. Death—Fiction.] I. Title.

PZ7.A3787Gho 2013

[Fic]—dc23

2012009887

FIRST
EDITION

FOR IRIS

GHOULISH SONG

FÍRST VERSE

THE LAST DAY OF Kaile's life did not start well.

She was up before the sun bothered to be, and fumbled a bit with her bedside lantern. The flint sparked, the wick caught, and she blinked herself awake in the sudden, violent light. Then she wound up the base and watched it turn.

The lantern was a music box, a shadow puppet show, and one of Kaile's very favorite things. Animals marched around the bedroom walls as it turned in a slow circle. She stared at the shadows while slowly remembering what day it was. She moved more quickly once she remembered, and scrambled out of bed. Ceramic floor tiles felt cold against the bottoms of her feet. Her own shadow climbed the wall behind her to join the marching puppets.

Kaile opened her window. She smelled coldness and wetness in the air outside. Her arms felt bumpy when she rubbed them, but she put on a simple work dress with short sleeves that wouldn't get in her way. Downstairs the oven was probably roaring. Downstairs it would be too warm already.

Kaile, the baker's daughter, closed the window and braided her hair by her reflection in the window glass. She hummed along with the lantern music, making it a tune to hold her hair together.

The music box wound down, and the lantern stopped turning. Kaile snuffed the wick and went downstairs.

* * *

A cloud of hot, dry air smacked into her when she opened the kitchen door. She had expected it, and was surprised by it anyway. The air also carried rich kitchen smells. It presented these various scents to Kaile with warmth and welcome. She breathed and sorted them, each from each.

Mother peered around the far side of the oven, which was a great, big, round, red mountain of clay with many doors and baking trays set into the sides. Mother's hair stuck up in strange places. It looked like someone had scrubbed the top of her head with the side of a sheep.

"Take out the first batch of breakfast pies," she told Kaile, without even saying *Good morning*. "They're nearly done."

Kaile grabbed a wooden paddle and braced herself for opening oven doors and breathing oven air. She tried not to be annoyed. Mother had probably not slept at all. She never did before Inspection Day.

Bakery inspections happened every year. The Guard Captain came, bought loaves of bread, and weighed them, one at a time, with his gearworked hands. If the loaves weren't heavy and substantial enough to pass muster—or if they weren't tasty enough—then the offending baker got locked in an iron cage by the docks and dunked several times in the River. After that the baker remained in the cage, suspended over the water, so people could laugh and jeer and throw stale breakfast rolls. The dunking went on for three days. It taught bakers not to cheat their neighbors by skimping on the substance of their bread dough.

Kaile suspected that her mother actually loved Inspection Day. She made the best bread and ale in Southside—everyone knew it, and Mother liked to remind everyone of it. She had never been dunked in the Zombay River for skimping on her dough. Not once. So every year her unbroken record got longer, and the pressure to keep it got stronger. Some neighbors started to whisper that she was getting a bit too proud, a bit too cocky, and that every baker should be dunked at least once to remind them that it *could* happen to anyone. Wasn't it just about her turn?

Mother only ever smiled at the whispered spite. *Not me,* she would say. *Not ever.* But she wasn't smiling now. She made grumbling and muttering noises at everything she touched. Kaile didn't want to know what Mother was saying to the kitchen as she moved through it.

Together they covered a countertop with breakfast pies, and filled the open shelves in the oven with pans of bread dough.

"Where's Father?" Kaile asked.

"I sent him out to clean the public room," Mother said. She wiped her forehead with a rag. It didn't matter. It only seemed to move the sweat around.

Kaile had helped her father clean the public room the night before. She didn't point this out now. Instead she looked around to see what needed doing next. Inspections came only once a year, and the day went faster if she kept busy. Leftovers were also especially good after Inspection Day, so she had that to look forward to.

She checked the windows to make sure Southside dust wasn't getting through the cloth screen and mixing with the flour—which always happened anyway, but it was best to limit just how much dust got in the bread—and then she set to kneading dough. She hummed a kneading sort of tune to herself. The tune gave shape to what she did, and held the whole of it together.

Kaile stopped humming and kneading when a shrill, piercing, horrible noise stabbed through the kitchen air. She covered her ears with both hands.

Now I have dough in my ears, she noticed. *I wonder if I'll be able to get it all out.*

"Wake up, everybody!" the Snotfish shouted. His name was Cob, but the name did not suit him nearly so well as Snotfish. "Inspection Daaaaaaay, Inspection Daaaaaaaaay..." He marched through the kitchen and blew another note into his tin whistle. The sound made it through Kaile's hands, and through the bread dough, and into her ears. It was even more painful than the first note.

Snotfish's whistle was his very favorite thing, and it had been ever since Kaile had given it to him in a moment of foolish generosity. It used to be hers. Now her little brother tried to play marching tunes with it, because the Guard used marching tunes to get used to their gearworked legs. He wanted to join the Guard when he grew old enough—if he ever did, if he managed to live so long before Mother and Father baked him into a pie to be done with him.

Kaile took her doughy hands from her ears and prepared to say wrathful and scathing things. She wasn't sure what she was going to say, but she took in a very big breath to make sure she would have enough air to say it with.

Her father was faster. He tore into the kitchen through the public room door and tried to snatch the whistle away. The Snotfish resisted, and the whistle spun out of his hands and into the oven fire.

Everyone started shouting at once.

The Snotfish ran to the oven with a shrill, wordless cry, ready to dive inside and rescue his precious whistle. Father grabbed the boy's arm to keep him from burning himself. Mother called down curses on the both of them.

Kaile took the longest kitchen tongs and tried to fish out the whistle. It was far inside. She felt the fine hairs burn on her forearms. A horrible, acrid, metallic smell began to fill the kitchen.

The shouting subsided. It was silent in the room by the time Kaile pulled out a ruined lump of tin.

She looked at it sadly. She should have kept it. She shouldn't have given it to the Snotfish. He never learned to play it properly, and now it would never play again.

Father brought her a water bucket, and she dropped the tin lump inside. Hot metal hissed and steamed. That was the only noise in the kitchen.

Mother opened the oven door and sniffed. She reached in with one hand, tore off a piece of still-baking bread, and took a bite.

"It tastes like tin," she said. She sounded calm. Kaile was a little bit afraid of how calm her mother sounded. "Tin does not taste good."

The Snotfish sniffed. Father's eyebrows scrunched together over the top of his nose.

"Both of you get out," Mother said. "Please get very far away from this oven."

Father and the Snotfish turned and left without further protest.

"Kaile," Mother said, her voice still very calm. "Fetch me more water. I need to make dough. Then take everything out of the oven and throw it in a crate for the guzzards, and after that open the public room. The old men are waiting already for their domini table, I'm sure."

"Yes, Mother," Kaile said, and left the kitchen. She was relieved to get away from the hot tin smell, and away from Mother's cold-burning calm.

SECOND VERSE

BROKEN WALL WAS THE name of the bakery, and the ale-house, and the neighborhood all around. Everyone drank ale in Southside. Well water needed to be boiled before drinking, or else it made the drinker's insides feel like a barrel full of angry fish, so it was very much safer to fill cups with fermented things. Light ale was practically water—only cleaner—and anyone could drink as much as they liked without getting fuzzy-headed over it. The darker, stronger ale was more dangerous. Only fully grown patrons could drink it, and they still needed Mother's permission before they could have so much as a sip.

Once she had fetched the water, Kaile took every last loaf out of the oven. Then she went quickly through the very clean public room, around the tall tables, and over the rope-woven rugs to open the front door. The domini men stood on the doorstep, waiting. They were four old sailors who rarely spoke. They had no beards, and they had no teeth except for the single copper set they shared between them whenever they ordered food—which was rarely. Mostly they drank light ale and played domini. Their fingers were like tree roots reaching down from the riverbank. Their skin was hard clay. Their domini tiles were yellowed bone, and they would keep up the game from now until closing time, when Mother would kick them out.

None of them thanked Kaile when she let them in, and they did not thank her when she poured ale for each at their usual table. They did not seem to notice her. They only noticed domini tiles.

Kaile wound up the gearwork charms beside each doorway, and hummed along with the jangling music they made. The charms were meant to keep illness, death, and malicious gossip away from the household.

She opened window shutters, and then lit a few lamps. Polished copper sheets behind the lamps broke their light into pieces and scattered those pieces around the room. She set the fresh breakfast pastries on the countertop—the ones that had escaped smelling like tin smoke—and stood behind them to wait for the breakfast crowd.

Familiar faces from the neighborhood stopped by for a bite, and Kaile sold them pastries. They stopped in for a quiet sip of a cold drink, and she sold them light ale. They stood at tables, or sat on the rope-woven rugs. They wore knit sweaters and coats stuffed with guzzard down because it was a cold morning.

Most of the patrons were rock-movers. This was the most common occupation in Broken Wall. They hauled the huge stones of the old city wall with levers and pulleys and gearwork and sweat to wherever those stones might be needed to build something else.

A small group of coalmakers came in for a drink. Their aprons and fingers were stained, and everyone else in the public room kept their distance from them. Coal came from hearts, removed and set to burning. Kaile sold them ale and tried not to stare at the stains on their fingers and aprons.

A few barge sailors came in with their hair in long braids. Kaile sold them each something to eat, and something to drink. She conducted the ordinary business of the morning, relieved by the familiar routine of it all, content that the day might turn out to be an ordinary day—notwithstanding the Inspection, and the panic, and the ruined slag of that tin whistle.

The public door opened again, and then it ceased to be an ordinary day.

A goblin strode over the threshold. He wore a trim gray beard, walked with a cane, and carried himself like a gentleman, even though he was clearly one of the Changed. He had very large eyes. His ears stuck out sideways from his head. He looked to be shorter than Kaile, though Kaile couldn't tell how tall the goblin really was underneath the enormity of his big black hat.

The old goblin looked around, nodded to the domini, men who were openly staring at him, and then recognized Kaile as someone who, for the moment at least, was in charge. He bowed to her with a flourish of his hat.

"Young lady," he said. The way he said it made it mean "lady who is young in years," and not "little girl." Kaile was impressed. She had only ever heard "young lady" mean "little girl."

"Welcome," she told the goblin, even though she wasn't sure that he would actually be welcome here, according to Mother or Father. But just at that moment, on that particular morning, it would be okay with her if goblins stole away the Snotfish and forced him into a hundred years of servitude, doing whatever goblins made stolen children do.

The goblin introduced himself. "I am the First Player of an acting troupe," he said, "the finest in all of Zombay." (Kaile couldn't tell if he meant that the *troupe* was the finest in the city, or that *he* was.) "We would be honored to perform for the entertainment and delight of your patrons. All the payment we ask is a hot meal, and whatever donations we earn from the crowd. There will be music, and mummery, and even masks."

Kaile imagined what her mother's reaction to this might be, and then tried not to imagine it. "I'm sorry," she told the goblin. "This isn't really the best day for a show. And the last time we had actors performing in here, the Guard tried to arrest them all. They broke furniture, and our oven. We had to spend days carrying clay up from the riverbanks to patch the oven."

The goblin made a sympathetic noise. "And what became of those unfortunate performers, do you know?"

"I don't," said Kaile. "One escaped through the kitchen. All the others were escorted out the front."

"I see," the goblin said. "I am merely curious about the fate of our predecessors. But I can assure you that *my* troupe has license to legally perform, without fear of harassment or arrest." He paused. "Well, truthfully, without fear of *arrest*. We are sometimes harassed, but we have very little fear of arrest. Hardly so much as a tremor of fear."

He smiled bravely, as if to show his courageous willingness to put on a show for the Broken Wall despite whatever dangers it might bring.

Kaile smiled back at him, but she also shook her head. Mother would bake her into a pie, and do it badly, and then throw the pie away as guzzard-feed. "We really couldn't," she told him. "Not today. Maybe another time."

The goblin nodded. "I understand, of course," he said, and swept off his hat to bow again.

Astonishing things fell out of the hat.

The first was a small mask with a pointy nose. The second was a gray flute carved out of bone. The third was a metal box. He quickly snatched up the mask and the flute, but the box he nudged with the tip of his boot, as though by accident. It snapped open. A copper flower, fashioned out of tiny filaments of gearwork, grew up from the box. The petals clicked against each other as it bloomed. Then it wilted. Each petal fell with a small clatter. The bare stem reached around the floor in an embarrassed sort of way, gathered up the petals, and closed the box lid over itself.

The goblin apologized, picked up the box, and hid it back inside his hat.

Kaile clapped. She couldn't help it. The domini men also clapped, all four of them, and Kaile had never seen them react to anything that was not their own tower of tiles.

"You can set up your stage on the long table at the end of the room," she said. She was in charge of the public room, at that moment at least, so it was her decision to make. "But not until the afternoon." The Guard Captain usually came to conduct his Inspection in the morning, and Father always took his shift during the midday crowd. Both should be over and done with by the afternoon. "Make sure it's me standing here at the counter when you come back, before you get started."

The old goblin winked. He seemed a trustworthy conspirator. "We will."

"And promise me you won't cause a ruckus and break the oven."

"The oven will suffer no damage from us," the goblin said—and more than said. He almost sang the words to make them more than just a promise, to change the shape of the world around them. Then he left.

Kaile heard domini tiles clack against each other. The day seemed ordinary again. She went back into the kitchen.

"Is the Captain here?" Mother asked. "The very best bread is in that basket, there by the door. That's the stuff to give him, if he's here."

"He isn't," Kaile told her, "but I'm running out of pastries. And I think it's Father's turn at the counter."

Mother grunted, handed over a tray of pastries, and disappeared behind the curve of the oven.

Third Verse

KAILE TOOK HER MIDDAY break outside, by the road, sitting on a broken piece of wall. She munched a pastry and watched people go by. She knew most of them, and most of them knew her. There was Old Jibb, who lost a leg to a dropped stone and had it replaced with one long, coiled spring. There was Brunip, who always walked with weights strapped to his left arm to balance out the mighty weight of his right arm, which was iron and bulky. Brunip took care of his arm, and scrubbed each individual piece every morning to keep the rust out. It glinted, shiny, when he lifted it to wave. Kaile waved back.

Rock-moving was dangerous. Many movers had replaced lost parts of themselves with gearworked fingers and toes. Their new bits were always makeshift and strangely shaped, pieced together out of salvage from old clocks or the rail station yard. Only the Guard Captain's hands looked like the hands he used to have. Only the

Guard used gearworked legs that would actually fit into boots.

Snotfish was several sorts of idiot for wanting to join the Guard, and get his feet replaced when they didn't need to be.

The Guard Captain—whose gearwork eyes always ticked in a cold, constant circle—was not here yet. The Inspection hadn't happened yet. It should have, by now. Goblins were coming to put on a show in the public room, and how had that ever seemed like a good idea?

Kaile frowned as she finished her pastry. It had too much redseed spice in it, which overwhelmed all the other tastes that should have been there.

She looked up and down the street for the Guard, or the goblin. She saw neither. The street was empty now, almost empty, which was a strange thing for this time of day.

Father opened the door and called for Kaile. Inside she went, nervous about goblins, nervous about Mother, and very nervous about the Captain of the Guard.

❋ ❋ ❋

Hungry patrons stood thick around the counter when the goblins returned, so Kaile didn't notice them at first. Five goblins came carrying boxes and crates filled with instruments, costumes, and masks. They made a makeshift stage at the far end of the room without checking in with Kaile, without giving her a chance to say, *Wait just a moment, the Inspection hasn't happened yet, so this whole business is no longer a good idea, if it ever was a good idea.* Then the juggling began, and it was too late to put a stop to it all.

The Snotfish crept out from underneath the counter. He had clearly been crying. His face looked like it was full of the stuff of his nickname.

"Those are goblins," he said, amazed. "The bald one's juggling."

"That's right," said Kaile. "Now please go away."

"Goblins *steal* you," said the Snotfish, with reverence and awe. "They steal you and turn you into a *ghoul*, with icky gray skin and no hair and no shadow, so then they'll have a whole army of ghouls and one day the Guard and the goblin ghoul army will *fight* and the Guard will have slings and crossbows built into one arm and swords built into the other arm that stick out like *this* when they move their hand like *this*"—he took an experimental swing; Kaile moved quickly, and rescued a pitcher of ale from her brother's sword-arm—"and they'll cut off seven ghoul-heads all at once, like *this*, and you'll get your head cut off because you'll be a ghoul, because they'll get you, because you let them in here!"

"Go away *now*, Snotfish."

He swung his imagined sword at her. "Ha!" he said, and ran under a table. That was fine. It was an empty table.

The juggler tossed green scarves in the air. He juggled the scarves in a swirling pattern that made him look like a tree in a windstorm. Then he started swapping out the green leaves for yellow and red ones to make autumn leaves. Then all of the scarves vanished, and he started to juggle metal bugs. The bugs flew buzzing in different directions, and they seemed reluctant to be juggled—one in particular kept trying to fly away from his grasp.

Patrons cheered—some for the juggler, and some for the bug—but Kaile couldn't pay too much attention. Too many people around her wanted ale and bread and meat pastries and sweet pastries. She brought them what they asked for. She glanced at the juggler every now and then to make sure he didn't knock over a lamp. She glanced at the front door, looking for the Guard Captain. She glanced at the kitchen door, looking for Mother. The afternoon was quickly passing by, and the Inspection had not happened yet.

A new sound startled her. The old goblin with the big black hat had begun to play a bandore. Kaile paused. She listened. She couldn't help it.

At first the notes sounded like laughter, like a quick series of rippling jokes. But under and around all that joke and tease was a slower, stronger current of music so overwhelmingly sad that Kaile almost left the room to get away from that bottomless feeling. It reminded her of Grandfather.

Kaile remembered how Grandfather would always play a tune in the morning before taking his bandore to his customary spot on the Fiddleway Bridge—a great big thing that spanned the ravine between the northern and southern halves of Zombay. Many houses and shops stood on that bridge, and the Clock Tower of Zombay stood over all the rest.

I'm off to hold the bridge together, he would say when he left. *It'll tumble down into the River without me.*

Kaile had believed him when he said that. She still believed him, a little, even though he had died several months ago. Even though his bandore had been buried with him. Even though the bridge was still standing without him. She supposed that there were other musicians and singers still on the Fiddleway, binding it together in Grandfather's absence. But she couldn't imagine that they managed it near so well as he had.

The music shifted, and a dancer stepped onstage. Kaile tried to watch the dance, but she was at the back of the crowd and behind the bakery counter, so she only caught glimpses of it. Each time her view cleared, another dancer seemed to have taken the stage, with a new gown, a new festival mask, and a new style of moving.

Some other goblin began to chant the story of *The Seven Dancers*, but Kaile didn't listen to the chant, only to the song, and she caught every note. The laughing and somber strains of music continued to weave around each other, but now the wildly skipping notes faded into the background. They must be getting to the sad part of the story. *The Seven Dancers* was one of the sad ones.

Whenever Grandfather came home from the bridge, he would sing songs that told stories about the bridge, and sometimes they would be sad stories—but even if they were, he would still sing them in a way that made Kaile and the Snotfish laugh. He sang about ghouls who haunted the Clock Tower, and about pirates who lived on the piers, and about the heartbroken girl who fell down from the Fiddleway and turned into a swan.

Sometimes Kaile accompanied Grandfather's playing with her own tin whistle, the one he had given her as a nameday present and taught her how to play. It was the one she had given to the Snotfish after Grandfather died, because she didn't want to play it anymore—the one that now sat at the bottom of a bucket as a ruined lump of slag.

Music ties knots, and unties them, he had told Kaile. *Think about a lullaby, one that ties up the world to make it a safe place for sleeping. It doesn't just convince the child—it convinces the world. Think about a funeral song. It can untie the string we use to hold our grief and let it all spill out. The same song, the very same song, can tie us back together again after we've spilled out.*

Kaile had listened. Later, at Grandfather's own funeral, she learned that this was perfectly true. But at the time she had laughed when Snotfish went on about the Guard fighting off armies of ghouls, and how ghoul-guts would spill everywhere. Grandfather had responded by strumming up a lively, ghoul-gut-spilling sort of song.

✳ ✳ ✳

Kaile shook her head to shake all those memories out of her thoughts and out of her ears. She glanced around the public room to see who needed their cups filled or their plates taken away. No one did. Everyone was listening. Everyone watched the dancing on the makeshift stage. Everyone clapped when it was over, and some threw coins. The juggler came out again, and he managed to catch the coins while still juggling other things.

Kaile clapped longer than anyone else, but she stopped when Mother came in through the kitchen door.

Mother stared at the stage for one long moment without blinking. Her mouth pressed together until it almost disappeared.

"Kaile," she said, "please join me in the kitchen."

Kaile joined Mother in the kitchen. It still smelled a little like tin. Father was there, holding water buckets.

"There are goblins on my table," Mother said.

"Yes," said Kaile. "I was—"

"There are singing, dancing goblins on top of my table."

Kaile tried again. "They asked if—"

"On Inspection Day," Mother went on. "There are goblins singing and dancing on my table, on Inspection Day."

"Yes," Kaile said again, trying to sound reasonable. "We don't have to pay them anything. Except for some supper. They just take tips from the crowd."

Mother turned to Father. "Throw them out, please," she said.

"No!" Kaile felt the skin of her face burning. This wasn't right. It wasn't fair.

Mother looked at her. Father looked at her and shook his head, warning Kaile not to face the floodwaters of her mother's will. Kaile knew this already. She knew better than to argue head-on with Mother. But she didn't have time, and she had made a promise, and the goblin with the big hat played bandore like Grandfather used to play.

She stood directly in front of the flood. "They aren't doing any harm."

Mother's voice became calmer, and quieter. "The Guard Captain is coming," she said. "My oven gets broken whenever performers and the Guard are both in my alehouse at the same time."

"The goblins promised they wouldn't hurt the—" Kaile started to say.

"And these actors are Changed," her mother said, as though Kaile had not said anything. "They might take you away. They might take your brother away."

Kaile, her mother, and her father all paused to think about whether or not losing the Snotfish would be a bad thing—but none of them joked about it.

"Please don't throw them out," Kaile said. *Grandfather's music is here now, even if he isn't.* "Please."

"Throw them out," Mother said. "They must be gone before the Guard Captain comes." She said it to Father, but she said it while looking down at Kaile.

Kaile tried desperately to think of something more to say, something that could change Mother's mind. She couldn't think of anything at all.

FOURTH VERSE

FATHER BROKE UP THE play. The goblin with the big black hat looked more affronted at the interruption, mid-song, than he did at the news that the show was now over.

Kaile stood seething in the kitchen doorway and silently agreed with the goblin. His unplayed notes seemed to hang in the air, or just on the other side of the air, frustrated and unfinished.

She listened to the goblin's sputtering outrage. She watched his companions hastily stuff their musical instruments, masks, and curtains into boxes, and carry those boxes outside. She didn't say anything. The patrons of the public room looked on as though this were just another part of the show.

Kaile went back inside the kitchen and let the door shut behind her.

Mother was there. She looked at Kaile and also said nothing. Kaile did not look at her. She refused to look at her. The show was over. The music was gone. The strum of bandore strings had sounded so much like Grandfather's own playing, and now it was gone.

Outside the kitchen window the old goblin began to curse.

"I will write you into our next play!" he roared. "I will sculpt your face into grotesque caricatures and paste them onto small, ugly puppets!" Kaile went to the window and peeked out. The goblin stood on the roof of their wagon and raged. "I'll pen your name into immortal verse, and for a thousand years it will be synonymous with ridicule and scorn!"

Kaile heard the door to the public room open and close again. She was alone in the kitchen when she turned to look. A basket containing the very best bread loaves—the ones meant for the Captain to weigh in his hands—sat on the table near the door.

"I will curse this place!" the goblin roared outside. "Your ale will turn! Your bread will be maggot-ridden! I will visit humiliations upon you in verse!"

Those were the sorts of curses that might stick. The goblin had promised Kaile only that he wouldn't hurt their *oven*, so there were all sorts of other aspects of the household that he could still curse without breaking his promise. Kaile made a decision. She told herself that it was a very practical decision as she made it.

She took the basket of bread, the very best bread, and went out into the yard.

It was raining. She hadn't realized that it was raining. She closed the basket lid and walked through the rain, which dampened down the usual dust-smells of Southside.

"May the River take you!" the goblin went on. "May the floods take your household and drown your bones! I will have our artificer build a pair of gearwork ravens, and they will croak your vile name outside your bedroom window, every night, at irregular intervals. You will never sleep again!" He paused. "Does anyone remember his name?"

Kaile did not want the goblins to curse her father's name. She did not even want them to curse her mother's name.

"Cob," she said, lying outright. "My father's name is Cob." All of this was the Snotfish's fault anyway. Probably. Sort of. Kaile still felt entirely awful as soon as the name was out of her mouth. Now goblin curses might come raining down on her brother to make him sick, or else lure him away to be eaten, or enslaved, or some other miserable thing.

The goblin climbed down from his wagon. Rainwater poured from the brim of his hat like a waterfall. "Cob," he said. "That is an easy syllable for a gearworked raven to remember and croak at him. What brings you out in the rain, Cob's daughter?"

"I'm just sorry he tossed you out," Kaile said, as cautiously polite as she knew how to be. "You should have some payment for the show, so I brought you some bread. It's fresh. It doesn't have maggots in it, not unless your curses work very fast." She gave him the basket, and all of the bread intended for the Captain of the Guard.

The goblin nodded. "I withdraw my curses on your household." He sang a tune to make it true. "I may yet carve a grotesque mask in your father's likeness, but I withdraw each curse. May the flood pass your doorstep and leave dry your boots."

"Thank you," she said, relieved that she hadn't brought any terrible curses down on the Snotfish. Then she paused, because she wanted to tell him about Grandfather and his music and how much it meant to her to hear echoes of his playing again. But she didn't know how to say that, exactly, or where to begin, so all she said was this: "The dancers were all perfect. Please tell them."

"I will," said the goblin. "But to whom should I attribute this critique? I have not yet caught your name, young lady."

It occurred to her that it might not be the best idea for a child to give her name to a strange goblin—there was no telling what he might do with it. But she decided that she didn't much care, and gave him the name her mother had given to her. Now he might work her name into a charm or a curse, but she didn't think that he would.

"I'm Kaile," she said.

The goblin bowed with another flourish of his hat. "Thank you, Kaile, for the tribute of your compliments and the bounty of your family's bakery." He reached into the hat and pulled forth the carved flute. "This token is yours, I think."

Kaile took the flute. It was a grayish yellow, and very light, and very smooth. She was about to say *thank you*, but then she heard shouting and hurried back inside.

Father stood in the kitchen doorway. He looked angry, and frightened, and even more angry because of how much he hated to be frightened.

"Your room," he said. "Now. Before your mother sees you. Best stay up there and out of the way."

Kaile went slowly up the stairs.

I've just given away the best bread in the house, she thought, and then she went more quickly up the stairs.

Kaile spent a long time thinking and pacing the length of her room. Outside her window the light began to fade. It was suppertime, but no one called her down to supper, and she stayed right where she was. Her stomach growled. She ignored it. She felt angry at her stomach for growling, and angry that she had helped make the day's food but hadn't eaten very much of it. And she was angry at Mother. She tried to think of all the reasons she could have for being angry at Mother, and she came up with so many that she made up a song to remember them all.

"Never says thanks, never combs her hair,
Never sings, never listens, and she doesn't really care
About anything other than a well-baked loaf,
And the oaf
Runs this place like a mean pirate skipper,
And she didn't even notice when I sorted all the flour. . . ."

She stopped. "Flour" and "skipper" didn't rhyme, not unless she twisted the word "flour" while she sang it. Kaile tried to think of other rhymes for "skipper." Then she gave up and examined her new flute, the goblin's gift. It had been carved simply and precisely from a single piece of bone. It was about the same size as the tin whistle that used to be hers, and used to be a whistle. The flute had no ornament, no swirly patterns worked into the side, no metal foil stamped on the surface. There was nothing fancy about the thing. It was just a bone with several holes— one for breath to go in, another for music to come out, and several for fingertips to shape the sound in between.

The Snotfish came into her room without knocking or asking her permission. Kaile hid the flute in a dresser drawer, but she didn't ask him to leave. She still felt guilty about redirecting the goblin's curses.

"What's that?" the Snotfish asked. He stood in one place, in the middle of the floor, shifting his weight around weirdly as though he didn't know how to stand in one place. Both his hair and his clothes looked embarrassed to be on him.

Kaile didn't answer, and she made it clear that she wasn't going to.

Little Cob Snotfish looked at the floor. He picked up one foot, held it with one hand, and put it down again. "Everyone's mad," he said.

Kaile nodded. She tried to smile in a reassuring sort of way. She didn't quite manage the smile. *I gave away the best bread in the house,* she thought, and tried not to think.

"The Captain came," the Snotfish said, suddenly excited again. "His hand folded back and he had the Mayor's stamp inside his arm to stamp the counter with." The Snotfish moved his own arm around to demonstrate. "Maybe he has a sword in his arm, too, right next to the stamp. Maybe it shoots out of his arm like *this* when he fights!"

"Did he do it?" Kaile asked, hoping to stall the inevitable

pantomime of combat. "Did he stamp the counter?" *Mother's second-best bread should have been good enough to pass.*

"His eyes went tick-tick-tick," the Snotfish said, as though that answered her question.

"Yes," Kaile agreed, trying very hard to be patient. "They do that. But did the Captain stamp the counter? Did we pass Inspection?"

"I got supper and you didn't!" her brother announced, gleeful.

Kaile stood up. "Get out of my room, Snotfish." He scampered out. She shut the door behind him, and then fetched the flute from its hiding place.

Kaile breathed into it. She played a single note. It was a sad note. It sounded like a breeze that would rather keep still, and never could.

She tried to play the tune she had just made up. Then she tried to play the music from *The Seven Dancers*, the one the old goblin had played on bandore.

The flute resisted both tunes. The notes all came out wrong. Kaile wrestled with it, trying to make the music in the room match the music in her head, but she couldn't manage to combine the two.

She let the flute have its own way. It played a song that she had never heard before. The notes of that song reso-nated inside Kaile's rib cage, making it difficult to breathe even as the music demanded more breath from her.

She played, and she kept on playing. The sound insisted that she hear it, that she understand everything it sang about. She didn't, and she was not at all sure that she wanted to. Kaile felt a shudder pass from her fingers to the tips of her toes. She stopped playing, and opened her eyes.

Mother, Father, and the Snotfish all stood in her doorway. She hadn't even heard the door open. Her family stared at her, and they stared at the wall behind her. All three of them looked stricken. Kaile began to suspect that they had not passed Inspection.

It turned out that they were worried about something else entirely.

"You don't have a shadow," the Snotfish said. "Only the dead don't have shadows."

FIFTH VERSE

MOTHER KNELT NEXT TO Kaile and checked to see if she was breathing.

"Of course I'm breathing," Kaile said. "I wouldn't be able to say anything if I wasn't. I wouldn't be able to play a flute, either." Her mother ignored what Kaile said, and checked the warmth of her skin, and looked into each eye without actually looking at Kaile at all—only at her eyes. Mother looked underneath each foot, where the lamplight couldn't reach, where the girl's shadow should still be hiding. She lifted them carefully, as though they were made out of breakable stuff. No shadow hid under her feet.

Kaile laughed, nervous and annoyed at the odd attention. She was not as worried about this as everyone else seemed to be. Her head was still in the music, even as the tune drifted away downstream to wherever music goes once played. She put the flute down on the chest of drawers behind her as though it were nothing important, as though it were something that she had certainly not received from goblins. No one else paid any attention to the flute. No one else laughed, either.

"Did we pass Inspection?" she asked, because she wanted to know, and because she wanted to deflect attention onto something that was not herself or the bottoms of her feet. Then she thought about why they might not have passed Inspection, and regretted asking. *The second-best bread should have been good enough*, she thought.

The Snotfish started to answer her, but both Mother and Father shushed him, and he let himself be shushed. Kaile was a little bit astonished that the Snotfish let himself be shushed.

"Send for Doctor Boggs," Mother said, "and for the witchworker."

"Where does the witchworker keep her shack today?" Father asked, already moving and not waiting for the answer.

"South of the rail station," Mother called after him, without facing him, without taking her eyes away from her daughter. Her voice was quiet, and quietly stumbled over itself. It cracked as she spoke. That never happened. It sounded like a crack in solid stone.

Mother wasn't angry. Kaile didn't know what Mother was, but angry wasn't it. Mother looked down at her daughter like she didn't quite know what Kaile was, either.

Kaile looked away. She kicked her feet against the side

of the chair. Then she stopped, because she didn't want to call attention to her feet and what was no longer underneath them, between them and the floor.

She wondered why Mother had sent for old Chicken Legs. They never had dealings with the witchworker. Mother didn't like heavy charms, or heavy curses—but maybe it would take a heavy charm to find a missing shadow.

She wondered where her shadow had gone.

※ ※ ※

Doctor Boggs hadn't paid a visit to Broken Wall since the Snotfish broke his leg—again—by doing exactly the same thing he had been doing the first time he had broken his leg. He fell from a crate stacked on top of another crate, which he had stacked on a table in the public room. He had been tying several lengths of twine to the rafters. Kaile didn't know why the Snotfish had been tying twine to the rafters, and she had never asked. Either he wouldn't answer, or else he would answer for hours and hours, and either way she would regret asking.

She heard Doctor Boggs arrive. He took a long time to huff his way up the stairs, and once in the room he paused to wipe sweat from his forehead. He must have run all the way from Borrow Street. Doctor Boggs was a wide man with big sideburns, and he wore spectacles in thin wire frames.

Mother moved out of his way. The Doctor knelt on the

floor. He focused his attention on Kaile without seeming to actually notice that she was there. Kaile looked back, her eyes full of questions that weren't asked or answered.

"She is not breathing," the Doctor said.

Kaile gasped, just a little. Then she coughed. She realized that she had been holding her breath. That made her laugh, again—a nervous sort of laugh that jumped out of her mouth before she could think to hold it back.

Doctor Boggs squinted at her, suspicious, as though he suspected Kaile of *pretending* to breathe. He checked her wrist with slow care. Everyone seemed so very afraid that she might be breakable. Then he sang a little tune. Doctors usually used songs to find the rhythm of a heartbeat, or tease out the shape of a broken bone, but Doctor Boggs's voice was painfully bad. Kaile wanted to cover her ears.

"Her heart is beating," the Doctor finally announced, "and she is warm to the touch—though if this has only just happened, then of course she would still be warm to the touch. Her skin would not yet have had the time to cool. And she has no shadow. That much is certain. That is the most important thing. She has no shadow at all." He looked under one of her feet, and then under the other, just as Mother had already done.

It was crowded in Kaile's room, much too crowded, too full of people who had barged in to examine her without looking at her, and to speak of her as though she were not there and listening.

One more followed.

A girl walked into the middle of the room. She looked to be only a couple of years senior to Kaile, but she acted very much older. Her clothes were dirty and badly patched, but she had an imperial way of standing. Kaile didn't like it. *This is my room you're standing in,* she thought, but did not say—and no longer really believed, because there were too many other people in her room and none of them had knocked before coming in.

Doctor Boggs stood up with a harrumphing noise. "And who exactly are you, young lady?"

"I am exactly Vass," said Vass. "You sent for a witch-worker. Graba's busy, and couldn't be rushed, so I'm the witchworker you sent for."

"I see," said Doctor Boggs. "Someone with more experience might be a little more helpful."

The girl Vass crossed her arms in front of her. "You don't see," she said. "Your glasses are broken, and cannot be mended."

Nothing at all happened. Doctor Boggs smiled. Then his spectacles slid from his nose, fell to the ground, and broke.

He made a quiet harrumph and began to pick up the pieces. "That was unnecessary."

Vass ignored him. She took a closer look at Kaile—and

actually looked at her, looked very much too closely at her. Kaile felt like squirming. She stared right back.

"Has anyone bothered to ask her how she lost her shadow?" the young witchworker said to the room, though she watched Kaile while speaking.

Mother looked as though she might answer. Doctor Boggs answered instead. "The unquiet dead must not be spoken to. And one can always spot the dead by their lack of a shadow. Those who do not properly touch the world always lack shadows."

Kaile turned her glare on Doctor Boggs. He was not actually a very good doctor. He had failed out of the medical school in Northside before setting up his practice south of the River, and he liked to *sound* right more than he liked to *be* right. But people in Broken Wall always listened to him, even if they made fun of him later. He was *their* doctor. He belonged to them, and he could set broken legs well enough, so they forgave him his bumbling and his stubborn, unfounded opinions.

"That right there is a load of impsense and grubbery," the witchworker scoffed. "Her heart beats. She's alive, whatever her shadow might be up to. That's the thing to concern yourselves with: her shadow, and why it left her. That's the thing to find out."

"Don't offer these good people false hope," the Doctor

snapped. "Once a shadow is gone, there is no calling it back again."

The young witchworker's eyes flicked over to the flute on the dresser, and then to Kaile. *Don't tell them,* the look said, clear as anything. *They'll take the flute away if you tell them, and you will be needing it.* Then she turned and left the room without another word to anyone. She had said what she had to say, and whether or not they listened was no further business of hers.

"What a rude child," said Doctor Boggs. Then he yelped and stuck his finger in his mouth, bleeding from a sharp piece of spectacle lens. He stood up, put the rest of the pieces he had found in a handkerchief, and tucked the bundle into his pocket. "I am very sorry," he said. "I know this is a sudden shock, and terrible, but you mustn't waste time if you mean to prevent a more serious haunting. We should speak downstairs."

He spoke to Mother, looked at the Snotfish, and gave a nod to Father in the doorway. He did not look at Kaile, or speak to her. The others followed him out of the room. They did not smirk behind his back, the way people always did whenever Doctor Boggs had been particularly useless, and they left the bedroom door open.

"Tell me if we passed Inspection!" Kaile called after them.

No one answered at first. Then the Snotfish stuck his

head in the doorway, whispered, "We didn't," and ran off.

Kaile stared at the open doorway. "The second-best bread *should* have been good enough," she said to herself.

The Snotfish crept back in. "Are you really dead?" he asked. Then he ran off again before she could answer.

Kaile closed the door, hoping that this would make the room belong to her again.

Someone climbed the stairs, opened the door, and returned downstairs. The footsteps sounded like Father's.

Kaile stared at the open doorway. "Never keep a door closed on a haunted room," she said aloud. It was something she knew. It was something that everyone knew. "The dead will never clear out if you keep the door shut."

She stood still for a moment. She could tell that her heart was beating by the way it pounded. She shifted her weight, and something tiny and sharp—a shard of Doctor Boggs's broken spectacles—drove into the heel of her foot. "Ow!" she said, loudly, and was suddenly furious. This was too much. Everything else she could handle, but glass stuck in her foot was more than anyone could reasonably be expected to tolerate.

She pried out the shard with her fingernails. Then she put a warm shawl on her shoulders, picked up the flute and her bedside lantern, and left the room that no longer felt like her own.

SIXTH VERSE

THE KITCHEN WAS EMPTY. Kaile fetched her rain boots from under the stairs, stuffed a piece of stale pastry in her mouth, and peered into the public room. The domini men still played at the usual table, but otherwise it stood empty of customers. Mother herself held a hushed discussion with Father and Doctor Boggs at the far end of the room, where the goblins had briefly set up their stage. They kept their heads down. The domini men also kept their heads down, focused on their game. One rattled the tiles in his hand as though more interested in the sound than in taking his turn.

"Drop those bones," another said, nudging him. "Drop those bones."

No one noticed Kaile as she slipped back inside the kitchen.

The stale pastry sat heavy in her stomach. "We failed

Inspection," she said to herself. She tried to wrap her mind around such a strangely shaped idea. Mother never failed Inspection. Something that never happened had finally happened. "It wasn't my fault," she said, her voice quiet and firm. "The Snotfish spoiled that first batch. I only gave away the second batch to protect all of us from curses—and it was Mother's fault that the goblins were throwing curses around, anyway. Their show was good, and the music was beautiful. They weren't doing any harm. She shouldn't have kicked them out."

Kaile's skin was angry and her bones were angry and her heart was angry, and also beating, so obviously she wasn't dead.

She left the kitchen through the back door and crossed the yard under a dim and dusky sky. Then she climbed up into the hayloft over the guzzard pen, where she used to hide when she was younger and less a part of the ordinary business of the day.

Some of the birds slept below while standing on one foot. Others made gurgling noises at her and hunched up their shoulders as if flapping wings that they didn't have.

The loft smelled like hay and guzzard. Kaile cleared loose straw from a patch of floor and set the lantern down. She sat beside it, turned the flint crank, and lit the wick. A warm glow filled the small space.

Kaile glanced at the wall behind her, where her shadow should have been. The lantern light passed right through her and left no sign that she was even there.

"Where did you go?" she asked.

Here, a voice whispered back.

Kaile jumped up to standing, and almost knocked the lantern over.

Be careful, the whisper said. *Don't put out the light.*

Kaile turned up the wick. "Who's there?"

She caught a glimpse of a wispy and indistinct shape near the ladder. Then she lost that glimpse, and had to squint to see it again.

Your shadow, of course, the shape whispered. Kaile thought she glimpsed a face and features as it spoke. It looked a little bit like Kaile's own reflection in window glass—but only a little bit. There was no shared movement and no spark of recognition, no sense that *This is me.*

"Tell me why you left," Kaile said. "Tell me why you aren't attached to my feet anymore."

I heard music, the shadow said. *It was beautiful and wrenching. It unmoored me. It cut me away from you. I huddled in our room while so many other people came in. Then they all left, and you left with the lantern. You left me almost in the dark. I followed. The only thing I know how to do is follow you. I don't want to. You never noticed me when you dragged me across the ground while walking. You never noticed when someone else stepped on my face. I don't want to be anywhere near you. But near you is the only place I know.*

Kaile wasn't sure what to say to all that. "I'm sorry if I splashed through too many puddles," she said. She wasn't sure she was actually sorry, though she tried to be. She felt as though she probably should be, but no one had ever told her to be careful where her shadow fell—and no one else ever seemed to care about their own. "I'm sorry, but I still wish you hadn't left. Now everyone thinks I'm dead. Or at least Doctor Boggs does. He thinks I'm a dead thing that won't stop walking around. A ghoul. He's probably trying to convince Mother and Father to hold my funeral already."

Sounds as though he managed it, the shadow whispered. *I can hear a funeral.*

Kaile listened. She held her breath to listen. She heard only guzzards. Then her ears caught the faint sound of a funeral song.

She scrambled for the ladder, leaving the flute and lantern and shadow behind.

* * *

The public room was packed. Kaile saw all sorts of neighbors and relations in the dim light, all of them softly singing. She hadn't seen the place so full since Grandfather's funeral.

Nice of you all to come so quickly, she thought, *but there really isn't any need.*

Grandfather's coffin had rested on the floor in the very center of the room, surrounded by candles. Kaile pushed her way through the crowd to stand in the center, where a small and empty coffin rested. It almost looked like a cradle, like the Snotfish's cradle when they had gathered around him to sing his nameday song. (Not that the name Cob had actually stuck.)

Kaile noticed in that moment that a nameday song and a funerary song had much the same shape and movement. That made a certain kind of sense to her. *You wave to say both hello and good-bye,* she thought. *The same motion means opposite things.*

Doctor Boggs stood at the head of the coffin, conducting the funeral. He took the lead with his terrible voice. The hair of his sideburns stuck out wide around his face, which turned ruddy colors when he noticed Kaile standing there. But he did not stop singing, and neither did anyone else. Heads turned halfway, startled, but no one looked at her directly— no one except for the Snotfish, and Mother gently reached down and turned the Snotfish away. Everyone looked elsewhere, pretending hard that Kaile was not nearby.

She almost laughed. She also felt panicked. What she really wanted was for everyone else to laugh. They all looked so stricken and serious. Mother and Father were both such sensible people. Why would they even listen to old Boggs? Couldn't they tell that she was still here and still breathing, still entirely alive?

The Doctor hit an especially bad note. Kaile winced. How could any of the dead rest in peace with a voice like that singing them down? Two fiddlers from the bridge had come to play and sing for Grandfather, and they had done so perfectly. Everything Kaile had felt on that day had spilled out into the shape of that music, and then the same music had tied her back together again—just as Grandfather had promised her. Now, at her own funeral, the music might just make her throw up. She wanted to leave. Maybe this was how the Doctor thought he could prevent a haunting: sing so badly that the dead were forced to leave.

Kaile was starting to think of herself as dead.

Stop it, she told herself.

"Stop it!" she told everyone else. "I'm fine. I'm right here." She needed to explain, but she wasn't sure how to explain.

The singing faltered and stumbled, but did not stop.

"My shadow's in the hayloft!" she protested. "If you'll all just wait a moment, I can try to coax her back inside. Just wait. Don't finish the funeral. Don't finish the song."

The singing grew louder to drown out her voice. Practically everyone she knew in the world stood in that room, and they all ignored her.

Kaile looked down at her feet. Without a shadow it seemed as though they didn't really touch the ground. It looked as though she didn't really touch the world.

She looked up at Mother. Mother was singing, even though she almost never sang. She didn't like the sound of her own voice. And Mother was grieving, actually grieving. This wasn't a punishment, not for goblins or inspections, not for anything. This was mourning.

They really did believe that Kaile was dead.

"I'm not a ghoul," Kaile insisted—but she said it quietly, because now she wasn't entirely sure.

Doctor Boggs gathered up a handful of greasy ashes from a bowl, took Kaile's arm roughly with his other hand, and smeared the ash across her forehead. He sang loud and only inches from her face. Then he pushed her through the crowd and through the public door.

No one else tried to stop him.

Doctor Boggs shut the door behind her.

Kaile heard the song and the funeral end on the other side of that door.

✳ ✳ ✳

She went slowly around the alehouse, across the yard, and up into the hayloft. There she sat with her legs over the edge and stared at nothing. Guzzards scratched in their sawdust below and dreamed the sorts of dreams known only to guzzards.

It could have been worse, her shadow whispered nearby. *It used to be worse. People used to bury suspected ghouls rather than just ignore them. They buried ghouls in three separate graves spaced far apart—one for your head, one for your heart, and a third for all the rest of you.*

"Shut it," said Kaile. She tried to wipe the ashes from her forehead. The ash stain was sticky. It smelled like they had mixed wood ashes from the oven with butter in order to make the stuff.

The stain marked her as a dead thing. She kept trying to rub it off.

"The funeral's over," she said. Her voice sounded flat and lifeless in her own ears. "My funeral song is over and sung. That makes it true. That changes the shape of things."

You aren't dead, her shadow told her. *Your breathing is obvious and loud.*

"Doesn't matter," said Kaile. "Everybody in Broken Wall knows that I'm supposed to be dead. It won't matter to them that I'm still moving and breathing and talking. They sang my funeral." She noticed, as though from a distance, that she was crying. She wondered how to stop.

You aren't dead, her shadow said again, with more impatience than sympathy.

"No help from you," said Kaile, as soon as she was able to say anything. "If you had stayed stuck to my feet, then this wouldn't have happened. If you had just come back inside with me, then it probably wouldn't have happened, either."

I don't want to be tied to your feet.

"Then why are you still here?" She heard another sob in her voice, and hated it.

The shadow's whisper faded, sounding embarrassed and barely audible. *I've only ever stood near you. That's all I know how to do. That's the only place I know where to be. I'd rather not. But I don't know where else to go. And it's dark outside.*

"That shouldn't much matter," said Kaile. "You're a shadow. You're made out of the dark. You shouldn't be afraid of the dark."

I disappear in the dark, the shadow lashed out, voice rising almost above a whisper. *It feels like drowning. I never know which part of me is me, or whether I'll ever come back again. I might not come back, now that I'm not anchored to you. But shadows are darker and stronger in bright lights. If that lantern burns out, then I might disappear and be forever gone. Turn up the wick as high as it goes.*

"No," said Kaile. "If I turn up the lantern, then the oil will burn out before morning. It needs to burn low if you want it to last until sunrise." She turned down the lantern wick. Her shadow made angry noises, but did not make any further protests.

Kaile wiped her nose, wound up the lantern base, and watched familiar animal silhouettes turn in a slow circle on the walls around them. Then she took another long look at her own shadow, which was easier to see now that Kaile had the knack of looking.

"What's your name?" she asked her shadow. "Do you have one?"

No, the shadow said.

"I have to call you something. I could call you Shade."

The shadow didn't agree. She didn't protest, either. She didn't say anything.

Kaile curled up in the hay, away from the edge of the loft, and tried to get comfortable. She wouldn't return to her bedroom, not tonight, not if her family had made her unwelcome, not if they wanted to keep the household free of haunting. Hopefully they wouldn't mind having a haunted hayloft.

She closed her eyes. When she finally slept, she dreamed that she was building the Fiddleway Bridge out of bones and bread loaves.

If Shade dreamed, they were the sorts of dreams known only to shadows.

SEVENTH VERSE

KAILE WOKE AFTER SUNRISE. Light came in through cracks in the walls. Guzzards went about their business below.

She felt like she had overslept. The sun rarely rose in the morning before she did. But she was sore, stiff, and cold from a night spent on unfamiliar and uncomfortable bedding—or else she felt stiff because she was dead, and her body had finally noticed. Maybe she would lurch around from now on, her arms and legs barely bending, the way the Snotfish did whenever he pretended to be something ghoulish.

She stood up, stretched, and paid attention to her own breathing for a while. Not dead, then—though her shadow was still separate from herself.

Shade crouched beside the lantern, a girl-shaped patch of transparent darkness. Kaile's eyes struggled to see the shadow, even though she was looking for her.

The lantern is almost out, Shade whispered, her voice a rebuke. *The oil barely lasted until morning.*

"Then it's a good thing I turned it down last night," said Kaile. "We keep a spare jar of lamp oil in the cellar. I'll sneak in for some breakfast and more oil. It probably won't take much sneaking—if anyone sees me, they'll just try not to notice me."

She kept her thoughts focused on practical things. Her thoughts and memories flinched whenever they strayed away from practical and ordinary things, and touched on the reasons why she had just woken up in the hayloft.

Kaile started to climb down. Then she paused. "Do you eat?"

I don't know, said Shade. *I used to eat the shadows of whatever you ate. Maybe I still can.*

"Easy enough," said Kaile. "Anything I find for breakfast should have a shadow of its own."

Kaile dropped to the bottom of the ladder and sneaked across the yard. She found the kitchen door closed and latched. A threshold charm made faint music behind it.

The kitchen door was never locked. Kaile hadn't even known that it could be locked.

She could still go around the whole building to the front door. That one would be open at this time of the morning—customers needed to get inside somehow. But

Kaile didn't move. The latch was a message: *Don't come back. Don't come haunting. You don't live here. You aren't alive. Please understand that you aren't alive.*

She almost kicked the door before she noticed the other message.

Someone had set a bundle of cloth on the doorstep, wrapped and tied into a satchel. Kaile picked it up and peered inside. She smelled the pastries before she could see them. They were fresh, and steaming, with just the right amount of redseed spice sprinkled over the glaze. She took one out and took a bite.

It tasted like a perfect morning.

A pair of neighborhood boys from rock-moving families passed through the alleyway. Kaile flinched, and looked for a place to hide, but they didn't notice her—or at least they pretended not to.

"Shouldn't feed the dead," one of them muttered before they turned the corner. "Shouldn't offer them a threshold meal. They'll keep coming back if you do."

Kaile almost shouted after them. She almost threatened to haunt them both. Instead she crept back to the hayloft with the pastries.

Shade sat in the largest shaft of sunlight with her arms and legs curled up tight against her. Sunlight passed through the shadow, but it made her darker and more solid-seeming, rather than diminishing her. *Did you bring lamp oil?*

"No," said Kaile. "I couldn't get inside. But I did bring breakfast."

She ate one full pastry and chewed it slowly, trying to savor the best of the early-morning batch. Shade reached over, hesitant, and took the pastry's shadow for her own meal.

Kaile wrapped up the rest of the food and tucked it into the satchel, along with her empty lantern and the bone-carved flute.

"We should go," she said. "Someone will be out here soon, to feed the guzzards and clean the stall. Probably Father. We shouldn't be here. I shouldn't be here."

He'll probably just ignore you, when he comes.

Kaile shook her head. "We should keep out of the way. And I don't want to be here. I don't want to watch Father ignore me." She felt embarrassed then. She felt like she had said too much. "Come on."

She slung the satchel over one shoulder and climbed down from the loft. Her shadow followed her around the alleyway and into the street—though she followed at a greater distance than she ever had before.

Other people were out and about, conducting the ordinary business of the day. No one looked at Kaile. They pretended not to see her. They walked wide around her. And they didn't seem to notice Shade at all. Kaile wondered why. The shadow seemed almost solid and embodied in direct sunlight.

You still have ashes on your forehead, Shade pointed out.

Kaile rubbed the back of her hand on her face. It only smeared the ashes around. The smear still marked her as the lead role in a recent funeral.

She started to panic, and rubbed harder at the ash stain. Then she forced herself to think practical thoughts. "Okay," she said. "First thing we need to do is find water I can wash my face with. Then we'll see about some lantern oil. Then we can . . ."

She stopped to watch a goblin walk down the street. He wore a mask with a crown, and he walked in an imperial and commanding kind of way. It made him look tall, even though he was in no way tall compared with the crowd of people who followed behind him. He also walked with a cane.

"That's the goblin who gave me the flute," said Kaile. "That was him. I'm sure that was him." She set off after the masked goblin. "His gift cut us apart, and I'd like to know why."

Shade walked alongside, keeping pace.

Watch where you step, the shadow whispered, reproachful. *Watch who you step on.*

Kaile tried not to step on other people's shadows as she walked. She really did try. But she kept forgetting to look at the ground. She didn't want to lose sight of the goblin.

* * *

The girl and her separate shadow followed the crowd that followed the goblin. They passed through Broken Wall and came to the edge of the River's ravine.

The masked goblin led them all down a steep, switchbacking road, down to the docks and the Floating Market— a set of narrow piers jutting out from the shore and over the River.

Kaile came here sometimes with her father to buy fish for the fish pies, and fruit for the fruit pastries, and spices to mix in with the dough or sprinkle over the glaze. Sometimes Father would offer Brunip a few free ales to push a wheelbarrow down to the docks and up again, if they meant to bring home more than they could carry by themselves.

She looked for her father in the market crowd. She didn't know what she would do if she saw him, or how she would feel. But she didn't have to find out, because she didn't notice anyone she knew—or at least no one she knew by name. A few familiar-looking faces passed through the crowd, but nobody here had attended her funeral.

They followed the goblin through the Floating Market.

Every barge tied up along the piers doubled as a market stall. The barge captains shouted, chanted, and sang about what they had to sell.

"Sugarcane and sea salt, good for charms and cooking!"

"Oceanfish! Riverfish! Dried and salted dustfish!"

An awning of glass and metal covered the market. Morning sunlight broke apart in the glass, and made strange shadows below.

It's too crowded here, Shade protested. *Everyone is getting mixed and mingled and stomped on.* She did a little hop-dance across the docks, stepping in sunlight.

"Oh, come on!" said Kaile. She wanted to be sympathetic. But she also felt much the same way she did whenever the Snotfish thought it was absolutely tragic that he didn't get to eat off his special plate with the blotch in the glaze that looked like a bird skull. *Just shut it and eat your dinner,* she always wanted to say to the Snotfish. *Just shut it and hurry,* she wanted to say to Shade. *This place is full of people, and I can't help where their shadows fall.*

"We have a goblin to catch," was all she said out loud. "Hurry."

She couldn't actually see the goblin, but she could still follow the press of people who followed him.

Kaile pushed through the market and down the length of the upstream pier.

Shade whispered unhappily at the thickness of the crowd as Kaile pressed through it.

Upstream mongers sold fine and fragile things, and the air smelled nice around their soap stalls. There was less singing and shouting at this end of the market, less bustle and noise. A few people glanced suspiciously at the determined girl in the simple work dress who had ashes on her forehead and straw in her hair.

The goblin's wagon floated on a raft at the end of the pier. One side of the wagon had been lowered to make a stage platform. The tallish juggler stood on the platform and tossed several silk scarves in the air, making a tree that burst into bright spring blossoms. People who had followed the old goblin down from Broken Wall now focused their attention on the juggler, and Kaile was able to make her way through. It was difficult to see. She found the goblin only by stumbling into him.

He lifted his cane, startled. Then he set it down again. His mask was stern-looking, and it glowered at her.

"Young lady Kaile," he said behind the mask. "My troupe and I very much appreciated your gift of bread yesterday. I am less appreciative of your clumsiness, however. Please excuse me. I must be onstage in mere moments."

Kaile grabbed his arm. Touching goblins was supposed to cause freckles, but Kaile wasn't worried about that. She had freckles already.

"You gave me a flute," she said.

"I did," he agreed. "You are welcome."

"It killed me," said Kaile.

The goblin looked surprised, or at least his posture did. She couldn't see his face behind the mask. "I find that somewhat unlikely, given the vitality of your voice and the strength of your grip on my arm." He tried to pull away. Kaile did not let go.

"It cut my shadow away from me," she told him. She looked behind her, but couldn't see Shade. "The shadow's around here somewhere—though seeing her is tricky, and no one else seems to have the knack. Now my family thinks that I'm dead, that I'm something ghoulish. They sang my funeral last night."

"Ah," said the goblin, a noise of understanding and sympathy. "I see. At least they didn't cut out your heart and send it downstream in a small paper barge. Such things have been done to the dead who will not keep still."

"Yes, I'm so very grateful," Kaile grumbled. "Now tell me why you cursed me with that flute."

"That flute was never meant to be a curse," the goblin said. There was genuine apology in his voice. "I am profoundly sorry that it seems to have become one. I merely recognized your grandfather in the way you carry yourself, and a musical gift seemed therefore appropriate. I had no notion that the gift would come between you and your shadow."

"You knew Grandfather?" Kaile asked, surprised.

"I did," he said. "I often heard his playing on the Fiddleway. He was a very fine strummer, one who held the bridge together, and the bridge is sorry to have lost him. It will be needing music of that kind one day soon. One *hour* soon, I think. The floods are coming."

"The floods are always coming," said Kaile. It was something people said, but it never seemed to actually happen.

"Indeed they are," the old goblin agreed, "and the time will soon come when they arrive."

He took a handkerchief from his coat pocket, handed it to Kaile, and gestured at her forehead. Kaile took the handkerchief and tried to wipe away the greasy ashes.

"I really must get onstage," the goblin said.

Kaile kept a firm grip on his arm. She didn't squeeze. Her grip was not the threatening, bullying kind. But she did not let go. "Tell me more about the flute," she insisted.

He sighed a dramatic sigh. Everything the old goblin did was dramatic. "I remember that I took it from a bone carver, here in this very marketplace, to answer a debt he owed me. Fidlam was his name. He is here today, I believe, and I imagine he would know more about the instrument and its history than I do. I suggest you go searching for him. I also recommend that you speak with the musicians of the Fiddleway, those your grandfather played alongside. They all know a great deal about songs and their effects, and might therefore know something about shadow-severing tunes."

"Thank you," said Kaile. She let go of his arm.

"You are most welcome," the goblin said, and straightened his coat and sleeve. "You might also try to discover whose bone that once was. It was a piece of someone before it played music."

He strode forward, stepped from pier to raft, and climbed onstage to address his audience in a booming voice.

Kaile took out the flute and examined it again.

Lots of ordinary things were made out of ordinary bones: needles and buttons, dice and beads. Mother had a set of spoons in the kitchen, all carved out of bone. Sailors made fishhook charms out of greatfish bones, and wore them around their necks to catch luck from the River. She assumed that most bone-carved things were made from sheep bones bought cheap at butchers' shops. It hadn't occurred to her to wonder what the bone had been before it was a flute.

The proper play began on the goblin stage, and the audience grew. Kaile pushed back through the crowd and went looking for Fidlam the bone carver. She also looked around for Shade, who was nowhere nearby. Kaile wondered where her shadow had gone now.

* * *

She found Shade beneath the Baker's Cage, and she found her mother inside it.

The cage dangled high over the crowd and over the River. Mother sat stoically through an especially vigorous pelting of stale rolls and bread loaves. She didn't see Kaile watching her. She didn't seem to see anyone. She held her head high and dignified, even as the winch dropped her between piers, even as it hoisted her, soaked and dripping, back above the heads of the crowd, who shouted, jeered, and threw more stale bread. Kaile was proud of her. Then she felt horrible about the second-best bread that put Mother in there. Then she she felt angry again. After that she didn't know what she felt, exactly. She wasn't sure how to sort feelings, each from each.

This is your fault, Shade whispered. There was no accusation in her voice. She said it as a simple statement of fact.

You're right, Kaile thought, but she didn't say that aloud.

A torn bread heel hit the side of Mother's face. Kaile couldn't keep watching. She turned away.

Mother's time in the Baker's Cage would continue for three days running, even though she was the best baker ever to punch dough in Southside, even though she had sung her daughter's funeral the night before. *They could have waited until she was done mourning for me,* Kaile thought.

Can we leave now? Shade asked, her voice small and strained. She had both shadowy arms wrapped around her shadowy self, and she was pointedly not looking at her feet. Other shadows came and went on the ground beneath them as other people arrived to throw stale bread.

"Yes," said Kaile. "Let's find you some oil for the lantern. And keep your eyes and ears open for a bone carver named Fidlam."

Shade followed close behind. *We don't have any money to buy lamp oil.*

"Then I'll play a song in trade," Kaile said. "And hope that playing this flute a second time won't separate me from my hair, or my toes, or something. Maybe I can just trade one of our pastries."

I don't think you can buy lamp oil for a song, said Shade. *Or for a pastry.*

"Then we'll spend all night under a streetlamp," Kaile told her, "just to keep you out of the dark. Now please stop whining."

They searched up and down the piers among

fruitmongers and clothmongers and clockmongers. Kaile asked questions. Sometimes people answered her, and sometimes they ignored her, but none of them had anything useful to offer.

"Brooches and buttons!" one scratchy voice called out. "Trinkets and beads! Dice and domini tiles! Catch the best luck, and catch envious looks, with Fidlam's fishhook charms!"

"Aha," said Kaile. "There he is." She made for the bone carver's barge stall.

Her shadow followed slowly behind her.

Fidlam was a tall man who wore a long squidskin coat. His pale eyes were set deeply in his face, and they had a hungry look to them. He had no customers at that moment, and the pier was empty around his wares.

Kaile stepped into that empty space and stood at the foot of the ramp. Shade stood beside her, but the bone carver only noticed Kaile.

"Welcome, young lady!" the artisan said, and smiled wide enough to swallow a pear without chewing first. "Young lady" meant "little girl" the way he said it. "Can I interest you in a fine comb? I have one carved into the shape of a leaping wingfish."

"No thank you," said Kaile, though she knew that her hair would disagree if it could speak for itself. She ran one hand over her braid, and picked out a piece of straw from the hayloft. "I was wondering . . ."

She paused when she saw the artisan's smile disappear, erased from his face. It left his jaw hanging half open. He stared at Kaile's forehead. He stared at her feet. Then he turned around, went inside the barge cabin, and shut the door behind himself.

"Mold, rot, and guzzard lips," said Kaile. "I still have ashes on my face, don't I?"

A bit, said Shade. *What now?*

"Now we insist that he answer some questions," said Kaile. "Even if he does think I'm dead." She marched up the ramp and onto the deck of the barge. Shade followed.

Display cases of carvings stood all around the deck. Kaile picked her way between the cases to the cabin door, and she raised one hand to pound on it.

She didn't actually get the chance.

The barge lurched. Carved bones rattled in their cases. Gearworks rumbled beneath them as the ramp and moorings withdrew from the pier.

Fidlam's barge made for the open River.

EIGHTH VERSE

KAILE FELL OVER BACKWARD. She shouted, alarmed. Then she got to her feet and finally managed to pound on the cabin door. It did not open, and she heard nothing from the man behind it. She gave up on the door, leaned out over the barge railing, and called for help. But the Floating Market was a very loud place, filled with shouting, singing, and the noise of goblins performing a play. Kaile's own shouts disappeared into that din, and no one else noticed.

The upstream pier, and the whole of the docks, slid far out of reach. Kaile stopped shouting to catch her breath.

We should have stayed on the pier, said Shade.

"You didn't have to follow me," Kaile shot back. "You don't have to follow me at all."

But I can't go my own way now, can I? the shadow responded. *We're both stuck here.*

"You can't," Kaile agreed. She was angry, and afraid, and angry about being afraid. "You can't go your own way, because a strange man with creepy eyes has abducted both of us and now we're stuck on his barge. If you can think of something helpful to do with yourself rather than sulking and disapproving, I'd like that very much."

She turned back to the railing and tried to figure out what she should do. Oars in the side of the barge moved like rippling centipede legs, pushing them into the River's central current. The air smelled clean and cold. She could still hear the noise of the docks and the city, the sounds skipping over the water's surface like flat stones. She tried shouting for help a few more times, and then gave up.

The River flowed strong and deep and wide around them. It had carved the ravine that separated the two sides of Zombay, water slicing through stone over hundreds of thousands of years. The current was very much too strong to swim through. Kaile knew that she couldn't escape by jumping overboard—not for very long, anyway.

She looked up at the towering pylons of the Fiddleway Bridge. Beneath them, Kaile felt entirely helpless and small.

She looked back at the docks, and saw the Baker's Cage dunked into the water and hauled up again.

She glanced around the barge deck, and at the display cases of carved bone. She saw a knife among them and picked it up. It was a delicate thing, with a landscape of trees and mountains carved into the side, and therefore not at all useful. She put it back.

The barge idled, its oars suddenly still. It was quiet out on the River and away from the docks. In that quiet Kaile noticed something she hadn't noticed before.

Dozens of windup charms had been nailed to the inside of the barge railing. All of them turned. All of them made small and jangling music, audible now that the oars had stilled themselves. Kaile listened to the tiny, separate tunes as they tangled up and tripped over each other. She recognized a few. Some of the charms were meant to keep away grudges, vendettas, and very bad weather. Most were intended to keep away ghouls.

"I've never seen so many windup charms in one place," she said.

I'm hungry, Shade said.

"What?" Kaile tried to concentrate around the jangling noise of conflicting tunes.

I'm hungry, Shade said again. *Could you eat something, so I can eat too?*

Kaile looked at the Clock Tower on the bridge, high above them and upstream. "It's midday," she said. "I suppose we should."

She set down the satchel and pulled out a meat pie, one filled with strips of smoked guzzard and good for a midday meal. She tried to savor it and gulp it down at the same time.

Shade plucked away its shadow for herself. She looked so solid in the sunlight.

"Why can't anyone else see you?" Kaile asked.

No one ever notices shadows, said Shade. *That's fine. I would rather not be seen by anyone but you. Your attention is bad enough.*

Kaile wished that she hadn't asked.

She stuffed the last bit of guzzard pie in her mouth. Then the cabin doors opened again, and the bone carver came out on deck. Kaile jumped up and tried to say something, but her mouth was still full.

Fidlam saw her, let out a startled yell, and stumbled backward. Once he caught his footing, he looked sideways at Kaile, and then quickly away.

"Shouldn't be here," he muttered. "All my little tinkly-tinkly charms should keep away one such as her. What's all this tinkling for if they can't manage that?" He moved around the deck, checking on the workings of his barge and winding up any charms that had wound their way down. He kept clear of Kaile, and his eyes looked everywhere but where she was.

Kaile swallowed the last of the pastry. She took the flute from her satchel and confronted the bone carver.

"You made this," she said. "You carved it. I need to know more about it."

Fidlam glanced at the flute and then away again. "Oho, *that's* the one you are. Thought it might be you. Didn't turn into a swan while falling down from the Fiddleway, did you? I wish you had. The songs say you were lovelorn and jumped into a watery rest for your broken heart, but not me. Never me. Always thought you were pushed, I did, and hoped the flute might sing a song of who it was that pushed you. Don't suppose you might just tell me, now that you're standing there? Who pushed you down from the high Fiddleway?"

Kaile noticed how much her heart was pounding. She tried to slow it down. "I'm not—that's a song, it isn't—I don't know what you're saying, but I'm not the girl you're mistaking me for." She held up the flute again. "Please, tell me whose bone this is."

Fidlam shook his head. "Your bone, of course. Traded it to goblins long ago."

"It's not mine!" Kaile insisted. "Not unless someone stole it and swapped it out for a stick of wood without my noticing, and I seriously doubt that."

Shade made a noise that sounded like a laugh.

Fidlam took no notice of shadow laughs. He turned away and continued to putter around the deck, tugging ropes and winding cranks. "Certainly one of her leg bones," he said. "And I'm not sure how she stands without it. Not sure how she's standing at all. Dead a long time. That's a long wait before taking up haunting. Must be that the floods are almost here. She drowned. She's one of the River's dead, and the River lets go of its dead in flood times. Loses track of them. If the drowned are up from their watery rest and walking around unquiet, then the floods are coming soon. If the floods are coming, then I'd best stash my wares and get myself downstream to safer harbor."

"Please make some sense!" Kaile shouted, frustration spilling over and into her voice. "Tell me where you found this bone!"

"Easy enough," Fidlam answered, still without looking at her. "The Kneecap's where we're going. We'll be there before the clock moves much."

❋ ❋ ❋

The River's Knee was a downstream bend where the River turned from flowing westward to flowing south. A pebble beach covered the northern shore of that bend. Sailors called it the Kneecap.

Fidlam drove his barge up onto the Kneecap with a scraping, grinding sound. Then he gathered his wares together: a comb carved to look like a wingfish in flight, several fishhook charms, the knife with a landscape carved into the side, a few simple pip-dice, two sets of domini tiles, and all sorts of other trinkets that Kaile didn't recognize. He shoved them into a large wooden crate, and then carried them down the ramp and onto the pebbly shore.

Kaile followed at a distance, cautious but curious. Shade followed Kaile.

The beach was a desolate place. Tree roots and branches, stripped bare and polished smooth, lay on the stones and grasped at the air. Living trees stood watch in a rim around the shore. They looked as gnarled and unforgiving as the driftwood. The steep slope of the ravine wall rose up behind the trees.

Fidlam heaved his crate of bones uphill, toward the trees and the cliff face. There, at the very base of the cliff, he kicked aside a few large pieces of driftwood to reveal a metal strongbox, chained and bolted to the ground.

"Here's where my wares will rest," he said. "No one else comes poking around on the Kneecap. No one but Fidlam. The sailors all say it's a haunted place." He laughed at that. "And it is haunted now, certainly, by one little ghoul girl—but the River will rise soon to take back its own. The drowned should stay sleeping in their own River bed."

Kaile didn't like the sound of that. "I didn't drown," she said with as much iron in her voice as she knew how to put there. "I'm not dead. It's just that my shadow doesn't like me very much."

Fidlam paid her no attention. He opened the strongbox and set the crate inside. "There," he said, talking to the box as he closed the lid and latch. "This beach is where you drifted with the driftwood, where you came to rest, before I made you into other sorts of pretty things. Now you'll all stay anchored here until the flood comes and goes. If any more of you start walking around to make unquiet mischief, you just keep that mischief contained to the Kneecap and off of my barge." He gave the lid an affectionate pat. "I'm off to race the flood downstream, but I'll be back for you after."

Kaile stared at the box. "You carve the bones that wash up on this beach." Most things that fell from the Fiddleway Bridge washed up on the Kneecap. Kaile knew that. Everyone knew that. "You carve the bones of *people* who wash up on this beach."

"And birds, and fish, and other things besides," Fidlam said cheerfully. "Though most birds and fish leave fragile bones. Not nearly so useful."

He looked at Kaile then. He actually looked at her with his pale and deep-set eyes. The look he gave her was curious and unsettling. She took a step backward, away from him.

"It was a good thing to meet you," he said. "If you can ever see your way to telling me who pushed you off the bridge, then I'll be sure to track them down—if they still live—and I'll give them a shameful shouting in some public place."

Kaile shook her head, frustrated. "We're not understanding each other here." She tried to think of a way to make him actually listen to her. "I'm not—"

Fidlam nodded in a formal farewell. Then he bolted back through the trees and across the beach, pebbles flying behind him. One struck Kaile in the eye.

"Ow!" She forced both eyes open and ran after the bone carver. Her sight was blurry, but she saw him climb the ramp and pull it up behind him.

The barge shuddered into movement, pushing itself away from shore.

Kaile shouted. She pleaded. She dropped her satchel, picked up a pebble, and threw it hard. She missed. The stone splashed and was gone.

Fidlam's barge sailed away downstream, leaving the girl and her separate shadow to haunt the River's Knee.

NINTH VERSE

KAILE ROLLED UP ALL of her fears and frustrations into one wordless lump of noise, and she shouted that lump across the River. Then she picked up her satchel and waved the flute over her head. "This was never my leg! I'm not dead, I didn't jump off the Fiddleway to drown a broken heart, and the flute isn't my leg bone!"

Shade's dark shape stood beside her. *You also haven't turned into a swan. It might be useful if you did, though.*

"I'm not a ghoul, either," said Kaile. "I'm not haunting Fidlam's barge, wailing ghoulish things and jumping up and down on his cabin roof to make sure he never gets any sleep ever again." She rubbed her eye, and then forced herself to stop because that only made it tear up again.

You're not a molekey, said Shade. *You're not anything that could scamper up the side of the cliff to get away from here.*

"I'm not a greatfish," said Kaile. "I'm not swimming in

the River. I'm not ramming the bottom of that barge with my tusks." She sat down on the beach. Pebbles crunched underneath. "I'm not anything useful."

Are you something that knows how to make a fire? Shade asked. *The lantern's still empty, and I don't think there's any lamp oil on the Kneecap. I don't know what'll happen to me when it gets dark. I really don't want to find out.*

Kaile noticed how cold she was, surrounded by River winds. She wrapped her shawl tight around her shoulders. "I'm a baker's daughter," she said. "Of course I can start a fire." She stood up, glad to have something to do, and began to gather driftwood into a pile. There was plenty of driftwood to gather.

Bones also lay scattered on the beach, but Kaile left those undisturbed.

She stacked large, small, and tiny sticks into a proper pile for fire starting, and then used the lantern flint to light it. The driftwood caught quickly. Soon she had a strong blaze burning.

"There," said Kaile, satisfied. "I've got warmth, and you've got light." She sat down beside the bonfire and felt the heat of it soak into her fingers, toes, and face.

Shade sat on the opposite side. She grew darker and stronger beside the bright flames. Kaile could make out the lines of her features.

The wood's burning quickly, the shadow said, sounding worried. *I hope we have enough to last through the night.*

"I'm sure we do," said Kaile. She wasn't actually sure. She had no idea how quickly they might exhaust their store of driftwood. But she was tired of her shadow's complaining. "Besides, we might not have to spend the whole night here. A passing barge might see the bonfire and come pick us up. Sailors are supposed to help the stranded."

Maybe, said Shade. *But this is a boneyard, remember? This is where pieces of the drowned wash up. Fidlam seemed pretty sure that no one else ever comes here. No one but him.*

"We'll shout for help when they go by," Kaile insisted. "Voices are supposed to carry across the River, as long as the River feels inclined to carry voices."

I'm sure that strange lights and shouting from a haunted place will bring us dozens and dozens of rescuers, said Shade. *I'm sure that will happen before the floods come and wash us away. I'm just sure of it.* Sarcasm smeared over her words like a glaze over sweet rolls.

"Shut it," Kaile said. "I bet it won't really flood. The floods are always coming, but they never really get here."

She watched the River go by. Then she examined the flute in her hand. Her fingers rested comfortably on the stops, as though each stop had been carved with her fingers in mind.

"Grandfather used to sing about the girl who jumped from the Fiddleway," said Kaile. "The one who maybe turned into a swan."

I know, said Shade from the other side of the fire. *I was there, too. I heard. I always listened.*

Kaile was uncomfortable with the fact that her shadow, which had always been with her, had always been listening—especially considering how sulky and disgruntled her shadow had turned out to be, now that they could speak to each other.

"Were you the girl who jumped?" Kaile asked the flute. "Was Grandfather playing your song? Did you get a bit cracked, and throw yourself down? Did you get your heart broken, and *then* go a bit cracked? Or did someone else push you, like Fidlam said? Did you wash up here afterward? Would you recognize that song if I sang it to you?"

The flute said nothing—unless a breath of breeze passing through it counted as something.

Kaile hummed the tune until the words of the first verse came to her. It was the only verse she remembered. Her memory caught notes and tunes more easily than it ever took hold of words and lyrics.

> *"A lovelorn girl from the long bridge fell*
> *To rest in the River's bed.*
> *A heart half-given broke her own,*

And words half-given broke instead.
Her mind half-muddled, she believed
She was a lovely, flying thing
And so flung herself down,
And so flung herself down,
And so mad Iren fell down from the bridge."

She stopped. The tune still broke her own heart a little, but she liked the girl in the song less and less the more she thought about the lyrics. She couldn't remember much of the second verse, in which Iren's fingers grew feathers while she fell.

"Do you remember a customer named Tacklesot?" Kaile asked Shade. Shade said nothing. Kaile went on. "A sailor. He used to come to Broken Wall whenever his barge came through Zombay. He told stories about sailors who despaired about one thing or another and then jumped overboard. Usually they drowned. The River isn't kind to swimmers. But sometimes they got fished out again, either by their own crew or by some other passing barge. Tacklesot said there's not a single living jumper who didn't regret the jump afterward—usually before they even hit the water. Each and every one of them said, 'Whoops, wish I hadn't done that.' I think he might have been one of the jumpers who got fished out again. He never said so, but I think that's how he knew."

Shade still said nothing. The fire snapped and crackled between them.

"Did you fling yourself down?" Kaile asked the flute again. "Did you say 'Whoops' afterward, before you hit the water, just like Tacklesot?"

Nothing and no one answered her. Kaile heard waves against the pebble shore. She heard a distant hum and buzz that might have been the Floating Market. She heard nothing else. She shifted her weight, uncomfortable sitting on small, cold stones, uncomfortable with no voices or music or movement around her. She was accustomed to the bustle, warmth, and company of her family's alehouse. The Kneecap was quiet, empty, and in every way different from Broken Wall.

"Can you hear me over there?" she asked her shadow. "Say something."

I can hear you, said Shade. *I've always heard you. I've heard every cruel and selfish thing you have ever muttered under your breath. I heard you yesterday when you tried to tell yourself that nothing was your fault. Mother failed the Inspection. Little Cob Snotfish almost had goblin curses called down on his little head. But that wasn't your fault. None of it was your fault. That's what you tried to tell yourself, and me. I can always hear you, but I don't usually believe you.*

Kaile sat stunned and perfectly still. Her face felt flushed and warm, so she turned it away from the fire and away from her shadow. She felt seething mixtures of anger, embarrassment, shame, and annoyance. Her fingers silently worked the stops of the flute. Then she brought it to her lips.

The first and last time she played this instrument, she had lost her shadow and found herself cast out of her home as a dead thing. She wondered what she might lose if she played it again. Maybe her hair. Maybe her toes. Maybe the music would sever her shadow so completely that Kaile would never see Shade again. Whatever it might do, Kaile decided that she didn't care.

She tried to play something that would have made Grandfather laugh, stomp his feet, and shout, *That's it! That will hold together!* She tried to play something that Mother might sing to, even though Mother almost never sang anything. Father had the better voice. It was Father who had sung lullabies at her bedside, or walked up and down the upstairs hall singing to the Snotfish when he was still tiny and hadn't learned how to sleep yet. But Mother would sing if the music was strong enough. Kaile tried to play something that would be strong enough.

The flute had its own will, and its own song to play. Every note took a step sideways. They shaped themselves into the very same tune from the day before, into the song that had rendered Kaile shadowless.

Kaile felt a quick stab of panic at the sound—but it was beautiful, and she reminded herself that she didn't much care what might happen. She played it through to the end. The notes went out over the River.

"Are you still there?" she asked Shade, once the song was done. She didn't look to check.

I'm still here, said Shade from across the fire.

Kaile was surprised to notice her own relief. She didn't want to be entirely alone, not here, not on the Kneecap.

Are you hungry? Shade asked.

"Not really," said Kaile, "but I'm guessing you are." She dug out the last of the pastries from home. Shade came around the fire, claimed the shadow-pastry, and then returned to her spot.

Kaile chewed a shadowless mouthful of cold crust and spiced potato. She stared out over the River, out at the passing barges that did not stop to investigate strange music and firelight. Then a fog began to rise and roll downstream, making it very much harder to see.

Rescuing sailors will surely find us now, said Shade.

"Shut it," said Kaile. She scooted closer to the fire as the air grew thick and dark around them.

※ ※ ※

The day cooled, grew stale, and ended. Clouds of fog and mist continued to hide both the far shore and the

Fiddleway upstream. Kaile could still see the glow from the Clock Tower, acting as a lighthouse beacon for sailors on the River. It felt strange to be marooned so close to the city, close enough to see and hear Zombay but still be stranded and very much outside. She added more wood to the fire, and noticed that the fire was gobbling up driftwood very quickly. She hoped it would last the night, but she knew it might not. Night had only just begun.

Something nearby made a knocking sound.

Kaile and Shade looked at each other.

"What was that?" Kaile asked.

It came from the trees, Shade answered. *It came from the base of the cliff. Night birds? Molekeys, maybe?*

The sound grew loud and pounding, like fists against a metal door.

That's the strongbox, Shade whispered. *That's Fidlam's strongbox, with all his carved bones in it. He said they might make unquiet mischief in flood time. He said the River dead get restless when the River's distracted by its own flooding. That's what he said.*

"This isn't a flood," Kaile insisted. "The whole Kneecap would be underwater if it was. We aren't in the midst of a flooding."

Words tumbled quickly through Shade's whispering voice. *A flood might still be coming. It might be soon. And the bones that wash up here are all people who drowned— people who jumped off the bridge, or were pushed off the bridge, or even just fell off the bridge by accident. Those who die before their time are the most likely sorts of dead to be unquiet afterward. This whole strip of shore might be haunted by them.*

Kaile glared at the foggy dark around them. "This place is haunted by *us*."

She said it to Shade, and to any other thing that might be listening. She tried to make it true as she said it. She tried to make this place hers, this circle of firelight her own, haunted by herself and her shadow and by no one and nothing else. She tried very hard to make that true.

All around them, from every direction, came a faint scraping sound. She saw movement by firelight, down among the pebbles.

The bones moved. They rolled and jumbled over the Kneecap, toward the trees, toward the base of the cliff where something pounded loud against the inside of Fidlam's strongbox.

Kaile noticed that she was standing, though she didn't actually remember getting to her feet. She noticed that Shade stood directly beside her rather than across the bonfire. She noticed the speed of her breath and her heartbeat, both of which insisted that she was not dead, that she was not haunting anything, and that no part of this place belonged to her.

Metal shrieked against metal as the strongbox burst open. The lid flew through the fog, over Kaile's head, and skipped across the surface of the River like a flat stone.

Shade screamed, a shadow scream unlike any sound Kaile had ever heard before.

The scattered bones moved faster now. They gathered together into larger shapes that rushed and scuttled like crabs across the shore.

Kaile stood with her eyes very wide open and her mouth pressed entirely shut.

What should we do? Shade whispered, over and over again. *What should we do?*

"Keep still," said Kaile. "Keep close to the fire, and keep very still. Whatever this is, it might not have anything to do with us. They might not notice us. They aren't moving in our direction, see?"

They're building on themselves, Shade whispered. *They're making larger things out of themselves. What should we do?*

Kaile tried to reach for her shadow's hand, but she found nothing solid to hold on to. She held the flute with both hands instead, and felt it tremble. It did not tug. It did not struggle to free itself from her grip and join the other bones. If anything, it tried to press itself more firmly into her grip. Kaile rubbed the flute with her thumb in what she hoped was a soothing sort of way.

A figure came walking toward them through the fog.

Kaile and Shade both moved around to the far side of the bonfire.

The figure was man shaped. It clattered and clacked as it stepped into the firelight. Its body was made entirely out of bones, and clothed in a tattered mess of riverweed and sailcloth scraps. It stood larger and wider than any living person. Many separate skeletons had gone into its making. Many bones had found new ways of fitting themselves together.

Several of the bones had been carved by Fidlam. Fishhook charms made up the curved nails of the figure's fingertips. Sets of dice clustered together as wristbones and knucklebones. Domini tiles made strange, huge teeth and protruded from the mouth of an ornately decorated skull.

The figure cast a shadow across the beach and away from the bonfire. Kaile almost laughed at the sight of that shadow. *Dead things* do *cast shadows,* she thought. *Doctor Boggs was so very wrong.*

The mouth of domini tiles opened. Noise clawed its way out. It was a raw sound, shaped by no lips or tongue. But Kaile recognized notes within that discord of noise, and she heard those notes gather together into the melody of a song—the same music that had severed Kaile from her shadow, the same song that her flute insisted on playing. But those very same notes sounded different now. The flute made them beautiful, wistful, and sad. The voice of this ghoulish thing made the song angry, vicious, and tormented. The ghoul screamed music. Kaile and Shade both cowered at the sound.

"We should run," Kaile whispered, though she didn't actually move. "We should be running. Right now. Very fast."

Nowhere to go, Shade whispered back. *Just a little strip of shore. And it's dark, too dark. I can't leave the fire. I'll disappear. I'll vanish in the dark.*

The figure drew slowly closer. The fire between them tossed sparks in the air.

"I wish I could just disappear," Kaile told her shadow.

No you don't, said Shade. *You really don't.*

The ghoulish thing sang instead of breathing, and its footsteps matched the beat of that song. The rags and scraps of riverweed it wore all knitted themselves together to the rhythm of its music. The bones fit more smoothly together to the patterns of its singing.

"The same song," Kaile said softly to herself. "The same song. The one stuck in this flute, stuck in all of these bones.

It binds itself together with that song." She had the spark-bright beginning of an idea. "You can't have more than one tune stuck in your head at once. There's only room for one." She turned to Shade. "Think of another song. Something catchy and annoying and impossible to get rid of."

Nowhere to go, Shade whispered, her voice very faint. The shadow backed away from the ghoul and the fire—but then she seemed to feel the darkness at her back, and stepped forward again. *Nowhere to go.*

Kaile made exasperated noises, and tried to think. Then she remembered "The Counting Song."

She had come up with the lyrics years ago, with some slight contributions from the Snotfish. He could barely talk at the time—and also couldn't stop talking. The Snotfish had laughed at every single rhyming word, and shouted those rhyme-words over and over again.

Mother had sent Grandfather upstairs to find them and quiet them down. Instead he had helped them shape the rhyme into a tune—a perfect, bouncing thing that lodged in the ears of anyone who heard it and refused to leave their heads for days and days. Patrons of the Broken Wall sang "The Counting Song" for weeks and months afterward. It was the single most annoying piece of music Kaile knew.

She sang it as loud as she could.

"One for the buns now overdone,
Two for the glue poured in your shoe,
Three for the pennies, haven't got any,
Four for the door in the hole in the floor . . ."

The ghoulish thing faltered, and so did its song. Kaile saw, and heard, the way that music gave it shape and held it all together. She poured more effort into her own singing voice.

"Five for the falling fisherbird dive,
Six for kicks and tocks and ticks,
Seven for the flour and the water and the leaven,
Eight for the grapes that I ate off your plate . . ."

The rags began to unravel. The bones began to scrape together, ill fitting. The ghoulish thing screamed its own music against the relentless and mercilessly memorable "Counting Song." Kaile shuddered and shrank back, but she also held her ground and her tune.

"Nine for your fingers tied with twine,
Ten for the guzzard hen shrieking, 'Again!'"

Kaile went back to one and the overdone buns, starting over.

The ghoul withdrew. It wrapped its raw and livid music around itself and retreated to the trees above the shore, away from "The Counting Song."

Kaile kept singing. She repeated the whole ten-count twice more before she let herself stop.

She could still hear the ghoulish song nearby, but it stayed where it was and came no closer.

She stood ready to sing again, if necessary.

She tried to convince her breathing to calm down.

"Well," said a voice behind her, announcing itself. "That was impressive."

TENTH VERSE

KAILE SPUN AROUND, SLIPPED on pebbles, and nearly stumbled into the bonfire. Adult-sized hands caught her before she fell.

"Easy there," said the strange voice. It was a woman's voice, though also deep and rough around the edges. "Be easy."

Kaile pulled free and pushed away. She had just faced down a ghoulish mess of many drowned remains, her heartbeat raged and pounded in her chest, and she was not in any way inclined to trust strangers who appeared suddenly behind her in the dark.

The stranger stepped back and put both hands in the air, a gesture of harmlessness and surrender. She looked like a sailor, dressed in oiled leather and squidskin. She had her hair tied up in several braids to keep the River winds from tying knots in it, and she carried a worn wooden lute case strapped to her back. Sunbaked wrinkles creased the skin around her eyes.

"Hello there," said the stranger. "I go by Luce Strumgut, and that's what you may call me. My barge is beached just a little ways upstream. I'm here to see if someone stranded and alive lit this here fire. Am I right in thinking that you're both of those things?"

"I'm stranded," said Kaile, "and I'd rather not be. But there's some disagreement about whether or not I'm alive."

Don't tell her that! Shade whispered nearby, her voice small and fierce. *She won't take us away from here if you tell her that.*

The stranger cocked her head sideways, clearly surprised. "You look living to me. Certainly compared to some. And I do mean to take you away from here, if you're willing to go."

Shade shrank away, putting distance between herself and the eavesdropping sailor. Kaile stared, astonished. "You heard her. I thought no one could hear her but me."

The sailor nodded. "I heard *something*, certainly—but it might not be my business to know what it was I heard. It's probably not my business to know what I might have just seen slink off into the fog and the trees. Whether or not you're entirely alive is *certainly* no business of mine. But regardless, you're welcome to follow me and climb aboard."

She turned around and walked along the shore, boots crunching against pebbles.

Kaile shared a look with her shadow.

Pick up a burning stick, if you can. I need light to follow, and the lantern is still empty. I need at least a little bit of light.

"I don't think she'll let me bring open flame onto a barge," said Kaile, but she took hold of a half-burned piece of driftwood anyway and used it as a torch. Then she gathered up her other few belongings in the satchel and hoisted it over one shoulder.

Maybe you should leave the flute here, Shade whispered. *It's from here. It washed up here. Maybe it'll make more unquiet mischief if you bring it with us. Maybe it wants to be a part of that other thing, that horrible thing.*

"It doesn't," said Kaile. "I'm sure that's the very last thing that it wants. I think we should keep it."

She held up her driftwood torch and followed the sailor, leaving the bonfire to burn itself out. Shade followed very close behind.

Kaile still heard snatches of ghoulish singing in among the trees. She walked faster.

A small and oddly shaped barge emerged from the fog as they approached. Lanterns burned at posts on all four corners. It had no enclosed cabin. A mess of machinery sat at the stern, and protruded from the sides.

Luce Strumgut climbed aboard without looking behind her. Kaile dropped her torch once safely near the lantern light. A wave of River water lapped over the stones and extinguished the tiny flame with a sharp, sudden hiss. Shade made an unhappy noise, but said nothing.

Kaile paused at the base of the ramp. Things had not worked out well the last time she had followed a stranger onto his barge. But she knew of no other way to leave the Kneecap, and she very much wanted to be far from this place and its unquiet bones.

She followed the sailor and climbed aboard the barge. Her shadow came with her.

"Welcome aboard the *Cracked Drum*," said Luce with a grand and mocking gesture. "It's not an inspiring name. It's not an inspiring craft, either, but luckily we haven't far to go." She pulled up the ramp with both hands, and then raised her voice. "Cymbat! We have a guest. One, at least. Possibly two, by the sound of them. Come introduce yourself."

A stooped and lanky figure came crawling out from behind the machinery. He did not look at Kaile, or speak to Kaile. He didn't look at Luce, either. Instead he focused on the gearworks, adjusting this and that with an oddly twisted wrench. The fingers of his free hand kept in constant motion, and tapped out a complicated rhythm against the side of his leg. Sometimes he squeaked and muttered to himself, but he made no kind of sense that Kaile could hear.

Luce pointed in his direction. "This is Cymbat, the cracked drummer—cracked like every other gearworker in Zombay—and the *Cracked Drum* is his craft. He's absolutely terrified of drowning, I can tell you—won't even *touch* the water—so I trust his fear to keep us afloat, if nothing else does."

I wonder what it was that hurt all the gearworkers, Shade whispered.

"Just working with gears did, I expect," said Luce. She didn't seem to notice that the shadow had spoken, and not Kaile.

Shade drew quickly away from the sailor, and away from Cymbat's frenetic motion, to crouch near the brightest lantern light. She clearly didn't like being overheard.

Luce took up a long oar and pushed the *Cracked Drum* away from the Kneecap. The bottom of the hull scraped against pebbles, and then they were free in the open water. Cymbat increased the pace of his tinkering. Gearworks whirred and ground together, turning pistons and propellers. Kaile watched him continue to tap out a drumbeat against everything he touched.

"You're both musicians," she said to the sailor. "He's a drummer. You carry a lute."

Cymbat barked a laugh without turning around.

"Well noticed," said Luce Strumgut. "It's true, of course.

We are both of the Fiddleway—and Fiddleway musicians have been searching for you since you played one particular tune yesterday, somewhere in Broken Wall."

The *Cracked Drum* turned against the current and pushed its way upstream, toward Zombay.

* * *

Kaile stood very still in the center of the barge.

"You've been looking for me." She was not at all sure what to make of this. "Since yesterday, you've been looking for me."

"We have," Luce said. "We don't actually know your name, though, so I'd be obliged if you finally introduced yourself."

Kaile did not introduce herself. "I was alone when I played that tune in Broken Wall. I was alone in my room. It used to be my room. It isn't anymore. How did you know? How could you have heard me? How did you find me now? And how do you know so much without knowing my name already?"

The sailor leaned casually back against the barge railing. All of her movements seemed casual. "That right there is a whole fleet of questions. I don't know your name because you haven't told me yet, even though I've told you mine—and also his." She nodded toward Cymbat. "That isn't very polite, but I don't begrudge your wariness. We did meet under strange and stressful circumstances."

Luce paused, expectant.

Kaile frowned. She wanted to *get* more information, and she did not feel inclined to *give* any. But the sailor kept waiting, so she said, "I'm Kaile."

"Hello, Kaile," said Luce. She paused again, still waiting, as though expecting Kaile to continue her introductions. But Kaile didn't look in her shadow's direction, and Shade made no noise at all.

"How did you know I played a tune in Broken Wall?" Kaile asked again.

"I know because I heard it," Luce told her. "So did every other Fiddleway musician. Some sounds carry. Shadows carry them. And I found you on the Kneecap because you played that selfsame tune again, and we all heard it again. Sound also carries over water, if the River lets it travel. So Cymbat and I hopped aboard this ramshackle barge and came to fetch you."

Cymbat let loose an indignant and gibbering sound.

"It *is* ramshackle," Luce insisted. "That's just about the kindest word I can use to honestly describe this craft. I've never sailed worse. It will take all the good luck that we three can pool together to reach the docks alive." She caught herself, and glanced at Kaile. "Forget I said that. I'm sure we'll be fine."

Kaile heard River waves smack against the hull, and

tried very hard not to think about sinking. She looked up at the foggy glow of the Clock Tower—the only thing she could see beyond the barge railing—but she couldn't tell how far away it was, or how much farther they had to go before reaching the docks.

Some sounds are carried by shadows, she thought. She wanted to ask more about shadows, and shadow sounds, and how someone's shadow might be severed by a song. But she didn't ask. Not yet. It felt cruel to call attention to Shade while she cowered in the corner.

"Why did you come to fetch me?" she asked instead. Then she wondered whether she should be so demanding of her rescuers, and if it might perhaps be a good thing to show more gratitude. "Thank you for doing it," she added quickly. "I'm really glad you did. But please tell me why."

Luce Strumgut gave Kaile a long look before answering. "The Master will explain it better, when we bring you to him. But I can tell you that only the very best musicians hear their shadows whispering. The first time any one of us plays a weighty piece of music, our shadow takes notice. Every solo tune becomes a duet after that, with shadowy accompaniment. And if someone can let loose a tune to catch the attention of every single musician's shadow in Zombay, then we take *particular* notice. We offer that someone the chance to audition."

The word "Master" sounded ominous to Kaile. She stared at the sailor, trying to judge how trustworthy she might be. In that moment, in the fog and the dim lantern light, Luce looked a little like a weatherworn version of Kaile's own mother. It made Kaile want to trust her—but the reminder was also an ache. It made her angry and sad by turns.

Kaile shook her head. Regardless of whom she might look like, Luce Strumgut was a musician of the Fiddleway. Kaile wanted a reason to trust her, and she chose that as her reason.

"My grandfather was a bridge musician," Kaile said. "His name was Korinth. He taught me how to play. He never mentioned auditioning, though."

"You had a good teacher," said Luce. "But he wouldn't have told you about this, not until you were ready. Are you willing to audition? I hope so. We did spend a lot of effort to find you."

Kaile was surprised to notice how much she did want to. She wanted to play beautiful music in the very same place where Grandfather had played. It would be like a conversation, every note an unspoken word. And if she had a place on the bridge, then she would have a place where she belonged. She wanted that so much that she had trouble breathing. But she also had doubts about shadowy accompaniment.

"I *can* hear my shadow whisper," Kaile said in a whisper of her own. "But she hates me. I don't think she'd ever accompany me on a piece of music. She doesn't much like my company."

Luce lowered her voice to match. "I did notice that the two of you walk around separately," she said. "I can't see where your shadow actually is, but I noticed where your shadow *isn't*. Never seen such a thing before, and I've sailed to just about every sailable place. How did it happen, if you don't mind my asking?"

"I played a tune," Kaile told her. "The one you heard. But my shadow didn't just notice. She left. She didn't go far, but she left, and now I'm dead. Everybody thinks I'm dead."

Luce snorted. "That's just a piece of silliness that people say, like thinking ruddy-haired folk bring thunderstorms when they snore. They don't. My late captain, eleven years drowned, had bright red hair and snored like a beast in pain, but storms didn't come thundering overhead any more often because of it. I am a bit concerned about the disconnect between yourself and your shadow, I won't deny that. Seems like it might cut you off from the world a little. But you're clearly not dead because of it. Don't worry about that. Too many other things need worrying about."

Kaile sighed relief. *She doesn't think I'm dead. She doesn't think I'm a ghoul. She isn't going to throw me overboard for haunting the barge. She isn't going to maroon me somewhere. She doesn't think I'm dead.*

The sailor looked thoughtful. "That ramshackle bone-house on the Kneecap was *certainly* dead, though. The one holding itself together with a song. And I *have* seen that happen before. Always in flood time. The drowned get restless at flood time, and the River gets distracted and loses its proper hold. And by the way, it was a piece of mad brilliance to throw a catchy counting song into the workings of its music."

"Thanks," Kaile said, and stood up a bit straighter. "I don't really know why it worked, though."

"You do know, more than likely," said Luce. "You might not have words for that knowledge, but you know it all the same. I once heard a pair of Northside scholars squabble about whether speech or song came first. Did the earliest people learn how to sing, and then eventually use their voices for more mundane things—or did they make words first and eventually learn to raise up those words in singing? On and on they fought over this, like children hurting their heads over riddles about eggs and guzzards."

"So what do *you* think?" Kaile asked, rather than trying to guess at it herself. The sailor clearly had an answer in mind and was itching to give it.

Luce broke into a sly grin. "The interesting question isn't 'Which came first?' Language and music were the very same thing in the long ago. I think it might be more interesting to ask 'Why did they split in two?' And I don't have an answer for that one. But here's the compass point of this chart I'm sketching for you: You can say with music what you can't say otherwise. You can understand with music what can't ever fit into words. And you can shape music to reshape the world, just as words do in charms and curses. Sailors learned that first." Luce proudly tapped the tip of her nose with one finger. "We sang chanties to the rhythm of oar and hoisted sail. It's madness to trust your own weight to a bit of bark adrift on water. It's only ever possible to face up to that madness with a song. So we made the music necessary to hold a barge together—or a bridge. The madness of the bridge, of walking and living and building whole houses high above the River, is only possible with *many* songs. You can hold anything together with the proper tune—or you can tear it apart."

Kaile mulled over the shape of these unfamiliar ideas. She listened to River waves as they smacked against the side of the hull.

Luce frowned. She cocked her ear to catch the same noise. "Flood's coming soon," she said. "Might even arrive tonight and smash this silly tub before we get back to the docks." She slapped the barge railing behind her. Then she looked sheepish. "Probably not, though. I'm sure we'll be fine."

The sailor took out her lute and played a cheerful sort of River chanty—something to hold the barge together. Otherwise they passed the rest of the trip in silence.

When Cymbat finally steered the barge against a pier, they docked directly underneath the empty Baker's Cage. Kaile peered through the fog to make sure it was empty. She was glad that punished bakers didn't need to spend the night caged. Mother would be back in it tomorrow morning, though—unless floodwaters came in the night and washed away the Baker's Cage first. Kaile hoped that that might happen.

"There," said Luce as she tied up the moorings. "Smooth as butter mixed with greatfish fat."

Then Cymbat turned around, caught sight of Shade in the corner, and started to scream.

ELEVENTH VERSE

THE SHADOW SHIED AWAY from the drummer and screamed back at him.

Luce dropped to a crouch and pulled a fish-gutting knife from her boot.

Kaile waved her hands in the air and shouted for everyone to please calm down.

It took a long time for this to happen, and even then the calm was fragile. Cymbat wouldn't go anywhere near Shade, or vice versa, and Shade wouldn't go anywhere at all without a steady source of light.

Luce agreed to bring a lantern, and took the largest one down from its pole.

"Do you have any spare lamp oil?" Kaile asked. "Ours ran dry."

"I'm afraid not," Luce admitted. "Poured the last of it into these lights this afternoon, when I felt the fog coming in."

Shade made an unhappy noise. She didn't say anything else as she followed Luce and Kaile down the barge ramp, carefully keeping inside the lantern's warm glow.

"Come on, Cymbat!" Luce called behind them.

Kaile heard the drummer squeak and mutter as he followed from a distance. She also heard the wood and metal sounds of barges rocking themselves to sleep at night.

Luce squinted, trying to see through the fog. "Few enough are docked here tonight," she said. "Good. Most of the captains must have gone looking for a safer harbor."

"What about the *Cracked Drum*?" Kaile asked.

"Not worth worrying about," said Luce. "It sinks all the time. Then the drummer spends a few days building it again. Now, let's see if anyone is still renting out carriages after nightfall. I'd rather not walk up the ravine roads myself."

Southside "carriages" were former wheelbarrows, built to move the stones of Broken Wall to wherever they might be needed—and then repurposed to move people around. Most had a simple wooden bench bolted into the wheelbarrow basin. Sometimes the benches had cushions on them, but usually not.

A carriage signpost stood at the base of the switch-backed road to Southside, and two wheelbarrows stood waiting underneath it.

"I'll need to rent them both," said Luce with a long sigh. "I don't think Cymbat will willingly ride in a carriage with your disembodied shadow."

Kaile said nothing. She recognized both of the wheelbarrow pushers, and both of them recognized her. Old Jibb looked quickly away. Brunip stared openly. He raised his iron arm a little bit, as though about to wave—but then Jibb kicked him with his spring-shaped leg, and Brunip let his arm drop.

"Hello, gents," said Luce, walking right up to them with a sailor's swagger. "I'll need to hire the both of you: one carriage for myself and the girls—and the *girl*, I mean—and one for the distracted fellow coming up behind us. Please take us all to the Beglicane house on the Fiddleway."

She gave each of them a bit of silver. It was more money than she needed to give, but it put to rest any objections that the two might have about carrying Kaile. Old Jibb still wouldn't look at her, though.

Luce climbed into the first wheelbarrow. Kaile followed, and Shade quickly and silently came last. Kaile sat in the middle, the sailor and the shadow to either side. Neither of the wheelbarrow pushers seemed to notice Shade at all—either because they couldn't see her, or because they were too busy not noticing Kaile by willful effort.

Cymbat settled himself into the second wheelbarrow, still grumbling unintelligible things.

Without a word, the wheelbarrow pushers set off. Old Jibb set a steady pace despite his spring-shaped leg.

"These two are from Broken Wall," said Luce, her voice low.

Kaile nodded.

"They know you," said Luce, "but they think you're a dead thing."

Kaile nodded again.

Luce snorted. "No tip for either of them—especially since I've already overpaid."

Kaile shook her head. "Not their fault," she whispered. "It was nice of them to come to my funeral."

"If you say so," said Luce.

The carriages climbed up the ravine and passed through the Broken Wall neighborhood, each familiar landmark made unfamiliar in the dark and the fog. They followed the winding and uneven Southside roads to the Fiddleway gatehouse, which always stood open. They passed under the gatehouse and onto the bridge.

The vast length of the Fiddleway stretched out over the River and connected the two halves of Zombay. Houses and shops lined the sides of it, and the Clock Tower stood over all the rest. Kaile could see the clock glowing through the fog above them. She saw lights flicker in a few house windows. She saw no one else out on the street.

This clearly bothered Luce. "Someone should be out here," the sailor said in an angry, worried way. "That boy with the glass harpsichord should be out here. It's his shift tonight. The flood is coming. We should have at least one musician playing at all times. Here I am, sailing off into the fog to bring us more auditionable material just so we can have every possible musician on deck, and now I find the bridge empty and silent. This isn't right. And I could swear I just heard a scraping sound. I should be hearing music, and instead I hear unpleasant scraping sounds. Did you catch that?"

Kaile listened, but she couldn't hear either music or unpleasant scraping sounds—only the metal-rimmed wheels of the wheelbarrow carriage as they fought with the road surface and found every bump.

"This is the place," Luce said loudly. "Drop us off here."

The wheelbarrows stopped beside a grand-looking house across the street from the Clock Tower. Kaile had seen the house many times, but she hadn't ever noticed it before. This close to the clock it was difficult to notice anything other than the clock.

The clockface showed a stained-glass landscape and thick glass clouds to match the actual weather. A glass moon passed through the clouds to show the time.

It was late. Kaile rarely ever stayed up so late, and this

particular day had been both full and strange, but somehow she wasn't tired. She felt as alert as a plucked string—though she also felt out of tune, and hungry. Her stomach complained.

Luce dismounted from the wheelbarrow. Kaile followed, and Shade came after.

The sailor gave her thanks to Brunip and Old Jibb, but she didn't offer either one of them a tip for their trouble. They both hurried away into Southside without complaint.

Kaile watched them go.

Luce took a key from around her neck and unlocked the great wooden door of the grand-looking house. "Come in, come in," she said. "Cymbat won't come near the entrance while your shadow stands nearby, and we've been out here in the clammy weather for long enough. Come in."

The inside of the house looked warm and well lit. Shade darted in first. Kaile followed. The grumbling drummer crept inside eventually. Luce came last.

The Beglicane house was large for a bridge home—large enough to have a full entrance hall with a sweeping double staircase carved in red stone. Cracks cut across the painted plaster walls and faded murals, but it still looked like a stately and respectable place. Candles burned in mirrored sconces on every wall.

"Welcome to the Beglicane estate," said Luce.

"Pegomancy Beglicane built this place a few hundred years back, when she grew tired of life as a pirate queen. She couldn't set foot on either side of the city, so she stormed the bridge, built the very largest house, and started the Fiddleway's sanctuary tradition. The Guard still can't place anyone in irons if they're standing on the bridge, and that was all her doing." She looked around, still seeming worried and disgruntled. "Where is everyone? Cymbat, find our guest something to eat. I can hear her stomach grumbling. I'll go check in with the Master upstairs."

Cymbat disappeared through a side door. Luce climbed the stairs quickly, her strides swallowing three steps apiece.

Kaile closed her eyes and took in a slow breath. She was welcome here. For the very first time since her funeral, she had been made welcome. She stood in a warm, dry place, far from the Kneecap and far from the hayloft she had woken up in. She soaked up this feeling and tried not to think about Old Jibb rushing off, bouncing with the uneven rhythm of his spring-shaped leg. She tried not to think about Brunip's bulk jogging alongside. Two familiar pieces of her own neighborhood had hurried away from her, and she tried not to think about that.

The drummer emerged with a small loaf of bread and a glass of very light ale. He didn't give them to Kaile. He set them on the floor nearby and backed away.

"Um, thanks," said Kaile. She picked them up. Shade reached out a tentative hand and took the shadows of the bread and glass.

Cymbat gave a yelp and hurried away again, leaving Kaile alone with her shadow.

This isn't nearly as good as Broken Wall bread, Shade whispered, chewing.

"Not nearly," Kaile agreed. Whoever had baked it hadn't bothered to cut gills in the top, so the finished loaf looked lumpy and awkward. It also tasted like dust and paper. She devoured it anyway. The light ale was refreshing, at least—though of course Mother's brew tasted very much better.

"They want me to audition," she said aloud, tasting the idea. "They want me to play for the bridge."

I hope you get to, Shade whispered. *But you probably won't.*

"What makes you say that?" Kaile demanded. "I played a tune that every bridge musician heard. I chased a ghoulish thing away with a counting song."

An annoying counting song, said Shade.

"That was the point. That's why it worked."

This will be different.

"How?" Kaile asked, but Shade finished the crumbs of her shadow-bread in silence and then changed the subject.

I wonder where that ghoulish thing is.

"It's probably still on the Kneecap," said Kaile. "No passing barge will give it a lift, not willingly. It'll pace around and sing to itself until the River rises and puts the drowned things back to bed."

You don't know that, said Shade. *You have no way of knowing that. You're just making up something comforting.*

"Of course I am," Kaile admitted. "But it won't work if you point out that that's what I'm doing."

I can't help it, said Shade. *I hear the flummery and bluster in your voice, and I can't help but point it out. I always have—you just never paid attention before. Go back to ignoring me if you'd rather.*

Kaile had been feeling rather confident about her audition, but Shade made that confidence collapse like a soufflé stabbed with a sharp stick. Kaile felt an ache where confidence used to be.

"Go away," she snapped. "Get away from me. Go cower in some little patch of candlelight."

Kaile stalked away from her shadow and pretended to look at the wall murals. Most of them showed idyllic scenes of drifting barges. None of them showed the noise and smoke of piracy. Kaile supposed that the old pirate queen had had enough noise and smoke by the time she built this house.

She did not see Shade leave, but when she looked around, Shade was already gone.

Kaile felt one pure moment of nameless panic. It surprised her. She should have felt relieved to get a bit of a break from her shadow's disparaging whispers. She told herself to feel relieved. Instead she searched the room, looking for Shade.

Kaile barely noticed when Luce Strumgut descended the staircase.

"Time for your audition," the sailor said. "Nibbledy, the Master of Music and the Fiddleway Revels, will hear you now."

Kaile laughed a nervous laugh. "Nibbledy?"

Luce gave her a look that could cut glass. "That's his name," she said. "Don't laugh at it. Don't think of it as cute. You really mustn't think of him as cute. And speak softly in his company. Don't shout. He can hear you. He can hear everything. He can listen to a jig with one ear, a dirge with the other, and then play a third tune entirely. He's the Master, and he isn't cute."

"Okay," said Kaile. "He isn't cute. And he wants me to audition tonight? Right now?"

"Yes indeed," said Luce. "Right now. As you may have heard me mention once or several times, there's a flood coming. The Master says it won't come tonight, which is some comfort—especially since that boy with the ridiculous glass contraption, who should be playing tonight, is nowhere to be heard—but even so, we haven't time for piss-ing and whistling. We need musicians. If you're willing to come and play, then you should do so now."

Kaile followed Luce up the long staircase. She looked once behind her and saw several shadows, but none of them was hers.

TWELFTH VERSE

THE THIRD FLOOR OF the Beglicane estate was a single music hall. Curved walls and arches captured sound and held it humming. Instruments rested on stands and shelves, carefully stored at the far end of the room.

In the very center of the music hall stood a dais, and on that platform stood the Master of Music and the Fiddleway Revels.

He was small, very small, and entirely hairless. He wore a fine coat, well tailored. His head seemed large for his body, and his eyes very large for his face. Kaile thought that he looked like an infant—but one with long ears that came to sharp little points.

He's an imp, she realized—someone Changed as an infant child. He might be many years or centuries older than she was.

Nibbledy the imp looked adorable. He looked like the Snotfish had looked, when the Snotfish was still a sweet little boy (before he became the Snotfish). Kaile tried not to grin. She tried to be respectful and respectable in the way she stood, and stared, and almost grinned.

Three other musicians stood behind Master Nibbledy. Two of them held fiddles—a smiling woman with wild gray hair, and a younger man with wide shoulders, a thick neck, and very large hands. Kaile recognized them both. The two of them had played at Grandfather's funeral.

The third musician was the youngest of the three—though clearly much older than Kaile. She held no instrument, and looked like a singer. She also looked sour. Her mouth puckered to a small, unpleasant point.

"The fiddlers are Murt and the Lady," Luce explained in a whisper. "They duel every day for the role of First Fiddler, but so far neither has won it. The Lady is a descendant of House Beglicane, so this house technically belongs to her. And the singer's name is Bombasta. Those three will stand witness. Cymbat won't come upstairs at the moment, so we'll just leave him be."

The imp seemed to ignore everyone. He focused his absolute attention on the floor in front of him, as though that spot of floor was the only thing that mattered or could ever matter.

He's listening, Kaile realized. She wasn't sure what he was listening to, exactly. She strained her own ears, trying to hear what he heard.

Luce cleared her throat. "Master of Music and the Fiddleway Revels, I present Kaile, granddaughter to Korinth, who hopes to audition for Korinth's place on the Fiddleway Bridge. I will stand as sponsor."

The Master looked up. He focused his full attention on Kaile with wide and solemn eyes. He nodded.

Kaile no longer felt the urge to grin.

"Instrument?" the Master asked. His voice had a very high register, but it was solemn all the same.

Kaile held up her flute.

The Master held out his own hand. Kaile approached and reluctantly handed over her flute.

Master Nibbledy squinted. He put the instrument to one eye like it was a thin telescope. Then he held it up to one ear and tapped it with a fingernail.

"Made out of bone," Murt the fiddler pointed out. "You'd get a cleaner sound from metal, and a warmer sound from wood. No reason to use bone when there are better-sounding options."

"The very oldest instruments in the world are carved from bone," said the Lady. "They might remember much."

"Maybe the urchin stole that flute from the Reliquary," said Bombasta the singer. Her voice affected a Northside accent, and each of her words shot out like a poke in the eye.

"I did not!" Kaile protested, too loudly. Everyone winced. "I didn't," she said, much more quietly.

The Master returned her flute. His face held no expression that Kaile knew how to read.

Luce came to stand beside the Master. Kaile noticed that their shadows overlapped as though huddling and whispering together.

The sailor spoke, almost chanting, almost singing. "From this hall and this house a musician can hear the Fiddleway Bridge. She can hear it in those who cross. She can hear it in those who live and move in the houses and shops. She can hear it in the tocks and ticks of the Clock Tower. She can hear it as the bridge sways in wind and water. She can hear it in the hum and whispers of shadows. Heed your shadow."

Luce paused to glance at Kaile's feet. Kaile swallowed. She looked over her shoulder to look for Shade, but Shade was not anywhere in the room.

"A musician of the Fiddleway can hear and match the rhythms of the bridge," Luce went on. "In times of flood, every musician will gather and play for the bridge. In times of smoke and blood, every musician will stand in the midst of battle and play for the bridge. In times of earthquake, every musician will remain here to hold the bridge together. All of this will be asked of you."

The Master looked at Kaile with his wide eyes, waiting. The fiddlers looked at her with hopeful faces. The singer looked scornful, though she also looked as though that expression might be permanent.

Kaile swallowed against a dry, dusty feeling in her throat. She nodded.

"Listen," said the Master. Kaile listened. She tried to hear the rhythm of the bridge.

"It's late," she quietly complained. "No one's crossing the bridge. There isn't much to hear."

"There is," Luce whispered. "There always is. Match your tune to the bridge, and the city around it, and the River below. Keep them together. Keep them in the same song."

The Master held up one hand for silence. Then he turned and pointed to the Lady. She took up her fiddle and she played. Notes flew from her like weapons, like knives and darts, like the bared teeth of hunting jites—even though the Lady seemed to Kaile like a kind and squishy sort of person.

Master Nibbledy pointed to Murt. The other fiddler began to play. His fingers were thick. They looked as precise as heavy wooden clubs. But those thick fingers played like raindrops, or like dance steps at a wedding. The dancing notes were also weapons, and the two fiddlers dueled each other. Their duel filled the music hall. Kaile's ears almost caught how they also matched the echoing rhythm of the Fiddleway Bridge.

The Master waved his hand as though wiping a window-pane clean. The duel ended in a draw. All of their duels ended in a draw, apparently.

The Master of Music and the Fiddleway Revels pointed at Kaile.

She took a breath, and then another one. She felt entirely alone, and as anxiously eager as Mother always seemed to feel on Inspection Day. She tried not to think about Inspection Day, or Mother.

Kaile took up her flute. At first she tried to play one of Grandfather's favorite tunes, because she was auditioning for the right to play in Grandfather's place. But the flute resisted. It pushed each note sideways and into the only music it was ever willing to play—the same song she had played while stranded on the Kneecap, the same song that had severed her shadow from herself. She played it a third time, but this time she felt clumsy. This time the notes stumbled one after the other, unable to line up or coalesce. Kaile thought she could hear the low creak and thrumming of the bridge, but she couldn't quite play alongside it.

The song came to an end. Kaile lowered her flute.

There was silence. In that silence the Master shook his

head. His wide and solemn eyes narrowed. The Snotfish used to put on a similar look right before he pitched a raging fit. Kaile wondered how old the Master really was, and how many years of impish experience he had had to sharpen his own raging fits. Kaile winced and braced herself.

Master Nibbledy turned and left the room. Each footstep struck the floor as though trying to drive holes into it. Then he was gone.

Kaile stood in a small puddle of silence and disappointment.

Bombasta sighed. "In the old days we threw failed musicians into the River, to keep their discord from spreading and shaking the whole bridge down."

"Hush up," said the Lady. "I don't think that is really true." She gave Kaile a look that was probably meant to be kind and consoling, but it looked more like pity to Kaile.

"Her shadow isn't with her," said Murt. "I can hear some potential, and we do need more musicians, but she won't be any help to the bridge if she can't hear it properly."

Luce took Kaile's hand and led her away. "Come with me," she said. "Let's find you a room for the night. This place has plenty of them."

"Only musicians are welcome here," Bombasta pointed out with prickly words. "She failed her audition. She shouldn't be welcome."

Luce glared at the singer. "It's late," she said. "The girl gets a bed. She's welcome here tonight, and so is her shadow—wherever the thing wandered off to."

She led Kaile to a small room with a stuffed mattress, a lamp on the wall, a washbasin, and a chamber pot tucked under the basin.

"Here you go," said the sailor, her voice uncharacteristically soft. "I'll bring you a bite to eat in the morning."

"Thank you," said Kaile. She felt dazed, disappointed, and tired deep down in the marrow of every bone. She couldn't hear the bridge, or hold it together. She would not play in Grandfather's place.

Luce stood still and thoughtful, without leaving. "That song you played. Did Korinth teach it to you?"

"No," said Kaile. Her voice sounded dull and flat in her own ears. "No one taught it to me. But the flute refuses to play any other song."

"Oh?" the sailor asked, interested. "And where did this stubborn flute come from?"

"The Kneecap," said Kaile. "I got it from a goblin, and he got it from a bone carver, but the carver first picked it up from the Kneecap."

"A *drowned* bone, then," Luce observed. "A drowned bone, unquiet in flood time. And it will only play the one song—a very important song. Every Fiddleway musician knows that song. It's the one we play to hold the bridge against a flood. That's why it was so important to find you, with floodwaters currently thundering down from the mountains. Not just because every bridge musician and their shadow heard you play, but because you played *that* song. It binds together the stones of this bridge. And it can shake things apart just as well, just as it shook your shadow from you. That's why we're so careful about auditioning."

"Oh," said Kaile. She sat down on the edge of the mattress. "I'm sorry I didn't pass. You spent all that effort finding me, but nothing much came of it."

The sailor shook her head. "I'm certainly not sorry about spending the effort. Worth it just to get you off the Kneecap. But all of this still needs figuring out. A drowned bone strives to teach you the flood song just before the River pitches its own raging fit. That's important. That's not the sort of thing we should ignore. The bone must have belonged to a Fiddleway musician—it wouldn't know that tune otherwise."

Kaile held the flute and felt the stops with her fingers.

You might also try to discover whose bone that once was, the goblin had said.

"How can I find out more about its history?" she asked Luce.

"We should go to the Reliquary and pester a Reliquarian

for answers," Luce told her. "They know all there is to know about bones, and they might help you puzzle with this one. I can show you the way to the Reliquary in the morning. I'll do that, unless I'm very badly needed here."

"Thanks," said Kaile, her voice soft and tired. It seemed like the thing to say, but she didn't feel especially hopeful. She wasn't welcome on the bridge after all. They only let her sleep here because Luce insisted, and they would only let her sleep here tonight.

"Good night," said the sailor. She closed the door behind her, but it didn't latch properly. The door slowly creaked open again after the sailor had gone.

Kaile remained where she was on the edge of the mattress. She didn't stand up. She didn't close the door. *Shouldn't ever close the door on a haunting,* she thought.

She would not become a bridge musician. She would not inherit Grandfather's place. She would have no musical conversations with him, playing where he used to play.

She felt as though her very last tie to family and home had been cut. She felt as though she did not touch the world, and was not a part of the world. She felt as empty as her lantern. She felt like she was hiding inside her own bare skeleton. She felt like a dead thing.

Shade crept in through the open door, and came to sit beside her.

You didn't pass, did you? Shade whispered. *I'm sorry. I should have been there. I shouldn't have left you alone.*

"I told you to go away," Kaile pointed out.

I shouldn't have listened.

"You can't help listening," Kaile reminded her shadow. "You're always listening."

I'm sorry, Shade whispered. *I'm still sorry.*

Kaile took in a breath, just to prove that she could, and then stood up. "Stay near the hallway light." She extinguished the wall lamp, removed the oil reservoir, and poured it into her own lantern. Then she lit the wick, wound up the lantern base, and set it on the floor. Shadow puppets in animal shapes moved on the walls all around them.

"There," Kaile said, and closed the door. "That should burn until morning."

Thank you, said Shade.

Kaile climbed into bed, kicked off her boots, and curled up under blankets. Shade darkened the other side of the mattress.

Kaile wanted to sleep. She tried to sleep. She couldn't sleep.

"What would happen to you if the lantern went out?" she asked.

I don't know, Shade whispered. *Before, the dark always felt like drowning and sinking and losing the whole shape of myself. I hear that other shadows can swim through it, and visit each other, but I don't know if that's true. I never got the knack of swimming. I only sank, and waited for the light to come back so I could have shape again. Now that we aren't tethered to each other anymore, I might just keep sinking forever. And there are other things that move through the dark, like flickerbloods and brighteaters. There are huge, slow-moving things that swallowed their own names a very long time ago.*

A joke and a tease hid in the shadow's voice.

"What's a brighteater?" Kaile asked.

They eat reflected light, said Shade. *With sharp little teeth. Be careful wearing gemstone rings after nightfall, or you might lose a finger.*

"Right," said Kaile. "I'll try to remember that the next time I wear jewels. Are you making all of this up?"

Maybe, said Shade.

"Are you trying to cheer me up, or scare me?"

Maybe both, said Shade. *Or else maybe these are deep, dark secrets that we shadows almost never let the bodied people know.*

Kaile laughed. She couldn't help it. Then she yawned. "Go to sleep," she said.

She tried to do the same, but she asked more questions instead of sleeping. "Why do you think the flute will only play that one song? And why did that ghoulish thing on the Kneecap use *the same song* to hold itself together?"

Shade didn't answer. She snored a whispering sort of snore.

Kaile rolled over and struggled with her own exhaustion.

You can hold anything together with the proper tune, Luce had said, *or you can tear it apart.*

Thirteenth Verse

THE NEXT MORNING THE Beglicane household was all bustle and chaos. Kaile crept downstairs to see musicians of every kind jostling for floor space and trying to tune their instruments. Luce Strumgut stood on one banister of the staircase and shouted like a barge captain in the midst of a storm. Master Nibbledy walked stately among the musicians, checked the tuning of their instruments, and gave his own solemn orders—each with a single word.

He only ever spoke one single word at a time.

Kaile found a window and peered outside. The world seemed calm enough. Morning sunlight glowed and glinted, and the surface of the River drifted downstream in what looked like an ordinary way.

"Not sure what the fuss is all about," she said to Shade, who stood beside her. "I don't see any flooding. But everybody's busy, and we're as much in the way as a Snotfish in a kitchen. Let's just go."

Luce said she would take us to the Reliquary, Shade whispered.

Kaile tried to get Luce's attention, but the lute-playing sailor's attention had already split into several pieces. None of those pieces noticed Kaile.

The Master paid her no mind, either. The only one who seemed to notice Kaile was Bombasta the singer, who stood in one corner sipping tea and glaring. *You are not supposed to be here,* the glare said.

Kaile agreed. She did not like taking up space where she was not welcome.

"We're not supposed to be here," she said. "Let's go."

She picked her way between the drums and foldable harpsichords, dodged a fretful bandore player who kept trying to replace a broken string with fumbling fingers, and finally made it to the front door.

Cymbat the drummer suddenly stood in her way.

He looked directly at Kaile for one moment, and then mumbled unintelligible things at the empty space just above her head. He noticed Shade, and flinched away from her, but only a little.

"Hello," said Kaile, nervous and uncertain. "Good luck with all this."

Cymbat handed over a very small bundle made from a napkin tied at the corners. Kaile took it.

What's that? Shade asked.

"Bread, cheese, and two apples," said Kaile as she peeked inside. "He gave us breakfast."

She looked up to thank the drummer, but Cymbat had already disappeared in the bustle and chaos.

* * *

Kaile and Shade ate their breakfast and shadow-breakfast outside. It was early, so there wasn't very much traffic flowing over the bridge. A farmer's cart passed by, heading north. A boy in a coat very much too big for him came walking south.

Kaile wiped crumbs from her mouth and the front of her dress. "Come on," she said. "Let's find this Reliquary place ourselves."

We don't know where it is, Shade pointed out. *And we've never been to Northside.*

"Then we'll just ask for directions," said Kaile. She slung her satchel over one shoulder and set out. Shade followed.

They crossed the Fiddleway into Northside. It seemed like a different city entirely, somewhere very far from home rather than just the northern half of their own Zombay. The streets were smooth, the rooftops were slate tile rather than tin sheets and thatch, and none of the walls were falling down. Northsiders wore shorter coats, taller hats, and fewer colors than Kaile was accustomed to.

She felt uncomfortable noticing these differences. It reminded her that she did not know the whole of Zombay as well as she had always thought. She didn't know her own city. She felt unwelcome. The word "home" seemed like noise to her now, like a very small sound that made no sense.

"Look at all these people," she said to Shade. "None of them are neighbors. I don't recognize *any* of them. I don't know where they're going. There's so much happening at the same time."

Of course, said Shade. *This is a city. There's always more than one story unfolding at once in a city.*

People looked at Kaile oddly when she asked for the Reliquary, but they gave her directions and she followed them. She tried to move with purpose, as though she really did know where she was going, because she had heard that unattended children in Northside got rounded up by the Guard and thrown into orphanages.

Don't walk so fast, Shade protested. *We're not in the Guard. We don't have gearworked legs.*

"We're not dustfish, either," said Kaile. "We can't swim through dust and leap between the drift dunes. Not that there are any drift dunes here. I wonder how they keep the streets so clean."

We're still not molekeys, said Shade, *so we can't scamper over the rooftops and make hiding places with our teeth.*

"Not here, anyway," said Kaile. "All the walls are brick and stone. Painful to bite through. And we're also not . . ."

She forgot about whatever it was that they were not, and stopped to stare at the building in front of them. It looked like a great big jewelry box of pointy stone spires. A pair of bronze doors stood open, gleaming in the sunlight.

"I think this is it," she said.

Probably, Shade agreed. *The doors are made out of bronzed bones all stacked together. That's a pretty big hint.*

The two of them passed through the open doors of stacked bones.

Inside, the Reliquary was a place of thin stone walls, wide windows, and soaring vaults held up by painted columns. Each column had an arch carved into the side, and every open niche held a skull.

Kaile looked down at the glass-smooth floor of polished stone. She saw her own reflection in it, and Shade's beside her.

"Do reflections mind that we're stepping on them?" Kaile asked.

No, said Shade, without looking down. *From where they stand, they're stepping on us.*

A voice called out to them. "Who is there?" The sound carried, bouncing between the stone columns. "Is someone there?" Footsteps hurried across the floor.

132

Kaile suddenly wanted to hide. She spoke up instead. "Here! Over here."

A woman came hurrying toward them. She wore a crisp and formal blue coat, and kept her hair mostly short and oddly styled—or at least Kaile thought it looked odd.

"A guest!" the woman called out. "A visitor! Would you care for a tour? I am Contrivia Runcemore, the Reliquarian on duty today, and I would be very pleased to conduct a tour." Her Northside accent sounded sharp and precise in Kaile's ears.

"Um, yes," Kaile said. "I'd like a tour. But I'd especially like to know about carved flutes. Flutes like this one."

She held up the flute. Runcemore the Reliquarian looked down, smiled, frowned, and then tried to smile again.

"Of course!" she said, with aggressive enthusiasm. Her voice sped up. "Right this way. But first—first we must admire the atrium as we pass through it." She held her arms wide to encompass the entryway and all its many columns, and launched herself into a practiced speech. "The space around you is dedicated to the history of Zombay, and to preserving the relics of our most significant personages. The skulls here belonged to every Lord Mayor who has ever governed the city—excluding the current Mayor, of course. He is still using his skull. Along the wall you can see the hand bones of every Captain of the Guard to have served the city—*including* the current Captain. He was kind enough to donate his old hands after replacing them with gearworks."

Kaile glanced politely at the bones on display. Pieces of important people sat on velvet cushions within glass cases, gold boxes, and stone arches. Shade walked beside her, and did not look around.

"They seem like actors in pretty little theaters," Kaile said. She meant it as a compliment, but the Reliquarian scowled.

"They do *not* resemble theaters," she said. "What a filthy comparison. The theaters have all closed, and good riddance to them."

"Sorry," Kaile said quietly.

With obvious effort, the Reliquarian wrestled away her scowl and resumed the tour. "Down that way we have the Chamber of Grotesques, where we keep all sorts of monstrosities and misshapen bones, oddly changed—and sometimes Changed, even! We have two goblin skeletons, and one set of bones that I believe may have belonged to a troll. Over in that direction we keep the Chamber of Infamous Criminals, and the Chamber of Beasts. I maintain the Chamber of Beasts myself. We will pass through it on the way to the Chamber of Curiosities, where the carved musical instruments are kept."

The Reliquarian led them into a long chamber, smaller than the atrium but with much larger bones on display. She gestured proudly at the ceiling, where a greatfish skeleton hung suspended by several copper chains. Kaile hadn't known that any living thing could be so huge—or any dead thing, either. Each of its tusks was bigger than she was.

"I call him Bufkins," said the Reliquarian. "He is new to the Reliquary. I only just assembled him last year, and employed a gearworker for a few extra touches. Observe. . . ." She took a long pole from one corner, reached up through the greatfish ribs with it, and cranked hidden springs. The skeleton began to move. It swished its tail back and forth, and opened its jaws. The great old bones seemed to remember swimming. Then the gearworks wound down, slowed, and stopped.

"I should install a piece of coal in there one day," the Reliquarian said, wistful. "If we made an automaton out of Bufkins, then I would not need to do the winding up."

Kaile was horrified, both by the suggestion and the Reliquarian's casual tone of voice.

"But coal's made out of *hearts*," she protested. Only the nastiest and most brutal people arrested by the Guard were supposed to have their hearts cut out for coalmaking, but no one really believed that the coalmakers limited their craft to nasty, brutal hearts—no one in Southside, at least.

The Reliquarian pretended not to hear her, and the tour continued.

They passed the bones of different animals, most of them with long legs and large teeth, all put together and posed as though they remembered how to move. Kaile kept expecting them to. She imagined that each beast turned its bony head to follow her, that each one kept its empty eye sockets focused on her as she passed by.

"Are all of these skeletons gearworked?" she asked. She tried to make the question casual, unconcerned, and not at all nervous.

"Oh, no," the Reliquarian said. "Only Bufkins. It would be wonderful, of course, to make all of my charges move. They could bow to the Lord Mayor when he comes, or do little dances to music on important occasions. Others would move much as they did in life, to show us how they were once accustomed to moving." She stood beside the posed skeleton of a jite, its teeth bared and wings outstretched to look as threatening as possible. The Reliquarian posed herself, mimicking the jite and holding out the tails of her coat like wings.

Kaile wasn't sure whether or not to laugh, so she didn't.

The Reliquarian dropped her coat-wings, resumed a dignified posture, and led the way down a long, windowless passage. Here the walls were made out of arm and leg bones, hundreds and thousands of them stacked on top of each other as though a multitude of the dead had built a fort out of themselves.

Kaile hoped that none of these bones had drowned, and that they wouldn't make unquiet mischief.

At the far end of the bone-built passage stood the Chamber of Curiosities, which displayed bones carved into other things. Kaile saw a model barge, a miniature tree, and a ticking clock.

"Here we are." The Reliquarian came to stand beside a shelf of flutes and whistles. "Some of these are really quite ancient. This one here is a favorite of mine, covered with carvings in an old script. Shall I read it to you?" She squinted at writing scratched into the bone, and then closed her eyes and tilted her head backward. She stayed that way for one long, silent moment.

"Hello?" Kaile finally said.

The Reliquarian opened one eye, and closed it again. "Excuse me. I am helping myself remember this ancient language by pouring the liquid stuff of my thoughts from the centers of sensory perception to the mental place of memory. Philosophers assure us that this is how memory works." She cleaned out her left ear with one long pinky finger, opened her eyes, and began to read. "*'This leg belonged to Heris, and she the greatest musician to walk these hills. With* so much music in her bones, she desired to be a source of music in death.' That's a lovely idea, I think—though I shouldn't want to risk playing it to find out how much music is left inside. This is a very old relic, very old, and cracked along the side."

She set down the leg of Heris, and picked up another flute. "This one is more grim. The inscription reads, '*I played a happy and frolicking tune at the execution of my murderer.*' That sounds horrible to me, and not at all frolicsome. Let's examine something else." She set that flute aside, and took up a pair of ribs. "These are drum bones. You play them by clacking them together. I would try it, but they might snap in half. They are older than this building, you know, and they remember a great deal. Here, let me read to you what they say." She squinted and moved her lips for a while before speaking. "'*Mine is the rhythm makes the bone-house. Mine is the beat inside that house. Mine is the dance and the dark in between. Mine is the building and mine is the breaking. Mine is the shaping and severing song.*' There. What an intriguing bit of old verse."

The Reliquarian returned the two ribs to their shelf. "Now tell me," she said, sounding suddenly nervous, "what interests you so much about bone-made music?"

"I need to know more about this flute," said Kaile, holding it up again. "I need to know why it insists on playing only one song. And I think I should find out whose bone it used to be. I have a solid guess about whose it is, but I don't really know."

Runcemore the Reliquarian stood thinking. Then she reached out and took the flute away from Kaile.

"Hey!" Kaile protested.

The Reliquarian ignored her protest. "Come with me. Let's see what answers we can find in my laboratory." She moved quickly to a doorway on the far side of the Chamber of Curiosities. The door was thick, and locked. The Reliquarian unlocked it with one iron key, which she kept in her coat pocket, and descended the spiral staircase on the other side.

Kaile followed, still unhappy that someone else was carrying her flute. Shade moved beside her.

* * *

The staircase ended in a metal door and a basement room beyond it. The stone walls here were rough and unpolished, and the floor made up of dirt and sawdust. A workbench lit by several lamps and cluttered with odd instruments took up one side of the room. A blazing cast-iron furnace took up the other end.

The room was hot, oven hot, kitchen hot—only worse, because there were no windows, and because the place smelled like rust and ash rather than baking bread.

"So sorry for the lack of polish," the Reliquarian said. "I do need to tidy up down here. Now, let's see what we can learn. I'll need a pinch of fine dust from the bone to begin."

She took up a dull knife and scraped at the side of the flute.

"Stop that!" Kaile told her, shocked.

Runcemore flinched away. "I've only scratched it," she said, defensive and scolding. She collected the bits of scraped bone dust in shallow metal basin, rubbed a pinch of it between two fingers, and tasted it. Then she lit a candle, took another pinch, and dropped the dust into the candle flame. The dust made tiny flashes of light as it fell. The Reliquarian studied the flame, and nodded.

"Carved from the femur of a young girl," she said, mostly to herself. "She stood at the same height as yourself, more or less, and wore her hair in much the same way. It seems that she also had a fondness for figs."

"You got all that from burning bone dust?" Kaile wondered.

"I did," the Reliquarian said. "And I can also tell that the girl died by drowning."

"I thought so," said Kaile. "Iren drowned. She didn't really turn into a swan."

The Reliquarian made a scornful noise. "That's a foolish song," she said. "I remember that the girl was foolish, too, though she died a very long time ago and I did not know her well. She was northern, and from a very good family, but wayward enough to take up singing on the Fiddleway. She even took apartments there. No good came of that, of course."

The Reliquarian looked sideways at Kaile. "I thought you might *be* Iren, at first. You do resemble her."

Kaile took two steps backward. "Why would you think that? Why would you think I was her? You just said that she died a very long time ago."

"She did," the Reliquarian agreed. "But I'm not at all sure when *you* died, shadowless thing." Metal scraped against metal as the Reliquarian shut the door and brought down the latch. Shade made a very unhappy noise.

"I'm not dead," Kaile insisted. She gave the Reliquarian a fierce and challenging look, one with iron in it. She had sharpened this look with long practice. She had used it to banish drunken patrons of the Broken Wall such that they slunk away from the public room in shame.

Runcemore the Reliquarian did not notice Kaile's iron look. "How sad," she said. She did not sound at all sad— though she did speak very quickly, all in a rush. "I had heard that ghouls are often unaware of their own death, and carry the delusion that they yet live. This seems to be the case with you. Your lack of shadow leaves no doubt, however. I am not at all sure what one dead girl is doing with the carved fragment of another dead girl, but the dead's business is none of mine."

"Then give me back my flute," Kaile told her. "Give it back. I'll go away, and then none of this will be any of your business."

"I really cannot do that," said the Reliquarian. "I would prefer it if you just went away, but my own responsibilities are clear. I should add this specimen to our collection of carved flutes. As for yourself, there are rules concerning the dead who continue to move; very clear rules, and far more humane and hygienic than the terrible things they do in Southside. No beheadings, no separate graves for separate pieces. None of that."

She walked wide around Kaile, keeping her distance, and crossed the room to the great furnace at the far side. She opened the furnace. A wood fire blazed inside, and waves of heat flooded the room.

"We burn ghouls here," the Reliquarian said.

FOURTEENTH VERSE

KAILE RAN TO THE door and wrestled with the latch, but it was too heavy and too high up.

She turned to face the Reliquarian, whose dark silhouette stood in front of the open furnace blaze.

"Please don't," Kaile said, with pleading in her voice. "Please. I'm breathing and my heart is beating and I *do* have a shadow but it's just that she's standing over there though you probably can't see her because nobody except for me and the cracked drummer can see her and if you burn me then there will be no one to light lanterns for her because she's afraid of the dark so please don't do this!"

"I really don't understand what you're saying," the Reliquarian said, her voice still rushed and flustered underneath the words she spoke. "I wish I did, but I don't. And burning you is for the best. It might not seem that way, but a good, cleansing fire is the only sure method to help the unquiet dead find peace. Truly. You should thank me for this—though of course I'll understand if you don't."

The Reliquarian took a step toward Kaile. Then she paused and took a step sideways. Her free hand fiddled with the buttons of her coat.

"I'm really not sure how to go about this," she admitted. "I have heard that one should avoid being bitten by a ghoul, if one can possibly avoid it, so I would appreciate it if you did not bite me. Perhaps I should hit you over the head with something first, to make sure that you don't." She picked up a log from the woodpile beside the furnace.

Kaile looked around desperately for a weapon of her own.

Even armed, the Reliquarian still kept her distance. She took a small step forward, and paused again.

She's afraid of you, Shade whispered. *She's trying to hide it, but I can hear it in her voice. She's terrified. Don't plead with her. Frighten her. Threaten her.*

Kaile tried to clear her head and focus her challenging look.

"I can do worse than bite you," she said. "I can curse you."

"How vulgar," Runcemore said, dismissive.

Kaile forced herself to move closer to the Reliquarian, and closer to the furnace. "I can curse the whole of the Reliquary," she said. "I can wake every single dead thing you keep here, every grotesque thing, every beast and former Mayor. Bufkins will thrash his tail without any gearworked help. The jite will gnash its teeth. The hands of former Captains will crawl across the floor and come looking for your throat. I can do this. I will do this."

The Reliquarian said nothing, but she hefted the log in her hand like a club.

Kaile did not flinch away. She moved closer, within striking distance. She smiled to make sure the older woman saw her teeth.

"I could also sing them all to sleep," Kaile offered. "I could do that instead. I can do it without fire, without burning anything. If you give me back my flute, then I can use it to make the whole Reliquary rest peacefully. And after that I'll leave and never come back."

The Reliquarian looked thoughtful.

"It's your choice," Kaile said. She tried to keep her voice calm, as though it didn't much matter to her which way the old woman chose. "You can help your relics sleep, or else force me to wake them up. All of them. Your choice."

Runcemore lowered her club—though she kept it in her hand rather than returning it to the woodpile.

"I confess that I would find it distasteful to knock you over the head and stuff you in the furnace," she admitted, clearly trying to sound aloof. It didn't work. Her voice cracked as she stumbled over her reasonable words, and her hand shook as she held out the flute.

Kaile took her flute back, and then lifted it to her lips.

She played a few phrases of the flute's only song, slow and soft like a lullaby, doing her best to pretend that it would soothe and charm the dead back to sleep.

"There," she said, when she was done. "Now the others will keep still." She hoped that was true. She hoped there were no drowned bones in the building.

"Lovely," said Runcemore. "But I should probably still burn you. It would be the most hygienic thing."

Kaile was expecting the Reliquarian to waver. She smiled again, showing teeth.

"But we did make a bargain, of sorts," the Reliquarian hastily said. She crossed the room, moving wide around Kaile, and then unlatched and opened the large metal door. "Be on your way, dead girl. Please do not bite anyone."

Kaile and Shade both raced up the stairs, ran through the Chamber of Curiosities and the Chamber of Beasts and the atrium, and left the Reliquary through its big bronze doors.

✷ ✷ ✷

Once outside, Kaile paused to catch her breath. The cool air was a relief after the stifling heat of the furnace room.

Are you okay? Shade whispered nearby.

"I'm okay," said Kaile, and she was glad to notice that it was true. She shifted her grip on her satchel and flute. "And I play better music when you're nearby."

Of course you do, said Shade. *That's how it works.* There was warmth and a smile in her words. Then she took a few steps, and both the warmth and the smile vanished. Shade began to pace back and forth.

"What is it?" Kaile asked. "What's wrong? Is it something worse than genteel relic curators who want to burn me?"

It's started, Shade whispered, her voice urgent. *It's here. The flood. And there's music on the bridge—but the music won't hold it together. I can hear the flood and the music shivering in the flagstones, in whispers passed between shadows. I can hear it. We have to go back there.*

"We won't do any good if we go back," Kaile objected. "We're useless. We can't help. I'm not a bridge musician."

It's my fault that you aren't. I should have stood beside you at the audition. But I'm with you now, and we have to get to the bridge.

Kaile looked for the Clock Tower. She was annoyed to discover that she couldn't actually see it from where they stood—she didn't know the way back to the bridge without using the tower as a reference point. It should have been visible from every single part of the city—especially Northside. This was high ground, built up tall and proud. It looked out over Southside, and turned up its nose at the dusty smells of Southside. But the buildings were too tall, and every brick and stone wall stood stiffly beside the next one like Guard members marching shoulder to shoulder. Kaile couldn't see between them or beyond them. She didn't know how to get back. She felt hopeless, and sad, and tired. She felt like she needed to curl up and hide somewhere far away and safe from people who wanted to burn her for ghoulishness.

"I don't know the way," she admitted.

I do, said Shade. *I can hear it. I can follow the sound.*

She set out, and Kaile followed her shadow.

* * *

A gatehouse stood over and around the entrance to the Fiddleway, just as in Southside—but the Southside gatehouse always stood empty. Here several members of the Guard looked down from the parapets. Sunlight glinted on their weapons and their gearworked limbs, and they shouted at the dense crowd of people who crossed the bridge below them. Kaile couldn't make out what the Guard were shouting. It sounded like guzzard bulls squawking to her. *Notice me. I'm important. Squawk, squawk, squawk.*

The crowd underneath the gatehouse moved in only one direction. No one headed south. No one tried to cross the bridge. Everyone was leaving it.

Bells rang in the Clock Tower. Kaile had never heard the bells before. They only ever rang when something vast and terrible threatened both city and bridge.

Underneath the high sound of the bells Kaile heard the roar of the River's own voice.

She followed Shade. The two of them pushed against the current of people leaving the Fiddleway.

She looked upstream, and saw the River rise up and begin to climb the walls of its canyon in great, frothing waves.

She looked downstream, and saw the Baker's Cage.

Mother's still there, she thought. *Mother's in the cage in the middle of the flood.*

Kaile smacked up against this knowledge and stood suddenly still.

Hurry! Shade called, her voice as loud as Kaile had ever heard it. The shadow moved deeper into the crowd, zigging and zagging as she tried to avoid stepping on her fellow shadows. Kaile followed, and tried to do the same.

Mother's in the Baker's Cage, she thought, over and over again, to the same pounding rhythm as her footsteps on flagstones and her heartbeat in her ears. *Mother's in the Baker's Cage. Mother's in the Baker's Cage.*

If the bridge fell, then it would tumble over and fall on the docks, and on the cage, and on Mother in the cage.

They passed through the gatehouse and came to the Fiddleway Bridge. The crowd around them thinned as more and more people fled into Northside. The sound of bridge music grew louder. Every musician had remained.

The bridge needs music in the mortar, said Shade. *It needs a song to tell these great big stones how to shift their weight. But the music isn't working, not well enough.*

They found Luce Strumgut playing furiously on her lute. Bombasta sang just across from the sailor in a language that Kaile couldn't recognize. It was all the same song, the same one that the flute insisted on playing—but the singer's voice and the sailor's lute remained separate and refused to coalesce, even as they danced around the very same notes.

Great big stones shifted under Kaile's feet with a lurch and a scrape.

Bombasta's song faltered. Luce stopped playing to catch her balance. Then she spotted Kaile. Her eyes grew wide and startled.

"Take your grandfather's place," the sailor ordered, and began to play again. "No one else is there."

"She can't!" Bombasta protested from across the street. "She failed her audition!"

"The formalities don't much matter at this moment," Luce argued. Her fingertips strummed across strings. "You just keep singing."

Bombasta disagreed. "This is not a *formality.* That little girl can't hear the bridge, or her own shadow, well enough to play here. We're having enough trouble orchestrating as it is."

"Why are you having so much trouble?" Kaile demanded.

"We don't know," said Luce. "We have no idea. Now ignore the singer, and take your grandfather's place."

Bombasta made wide and frustrated gestures with both hands. "You aren't the conductor here! Nibbledy will pitch an absolute fit!"

"I've survived the Master's fits before," Luce calmly said. "And if we can't all play together soon, then none of us will survive the next hour. Stop talking and sing." Her fingertips picked out a quick flourish as she looked down at Kaile. "Girl, either get away from here and climb to the highest ground you can find, or else take old Korinth's place and play."

Kaile nodded. Then she ran. Shade ran with her.

"Heed your shadow!" Luce called after her.

✳ ✳ ✳

Kaile found the empty circle of brick beneath a lamppost. Grandfather had come here every day to play his bandore. Mother had sent Kaile to this spot with a warm pastry on cold days, because Grandfather would play without noticing his own hunger, or the cold. Sometimes Kaile had stood here for a long time beside him, listening, forgetting she had come for any other reason but to listen.

The bridge creaked and crunched again, struggling to hold itself upright against the rising floodwaters.

If the bridge falls, it'll fall on the docks, she thought. *It'll fall on the cage. Even if Mother doesn't drown in the flooding, she'll be crushed by the falling bridge. We have to hold the bridge together.*

She stood in Grandfather's place and tried to steady her own breathing. She would need a steady breath to play.

Wait, Shade whispered.

"Wait?" Kaile asked, incredulous. "You rush me out here, onto a bridge that will probably collapse and kill us both, and now you tell me to wait? There's no time for waiting!"

The music isn't working, you silly sack of guzzard gizzards. Shade sharpened each word and poked them at Kaile. *I can hear how it isn't working. I can hear why. Listen. Not to me. Don't listen to me. Listen!*

Kaile listened. She heard musicians of every kind. She heard them sing and play to the north and the south. She heard them struggle with a song whose separate fragments stubbornly refused to combine into a single piece of music.

Then she heard discord. She heard one strain of the song work against the others, forcing them apart. And she heard what direction that discord was coming from.

"There," she said, pointing at a rough and battered house across the street. It looked abandoned. The door and the windows were all boarded up.

There, Shade agreed.

The doorway had been sealed a very long time ago, and not very well. Rotting boards crumbled when Kaile pulled them away, and rusty nails broke in half. The latch also broke when she shoved hard against the door with her shoulder.

Kaile crossed the threshold.

The flute flinched in her hand.

She looked around, startled. The inside of the house was flame-charred and empty.

"The flute knows this place," she said.

Light the lantern, Shade whispered behind her. *It's too dark in there for me.*

Kaile fiddled with the lantern flint. "Not much oil left from last night," she said, worried. The wick still caught. Shadow puppets leaped out across the soot-stained walls.

One shadow stepped out of the dark and stood separate in front of them, confronting them both.

You have a piece of her, this shadow whispered. *You're carrying a piece of her.*

"Who are you?" Kaile whispered back—but it was Shade who answered.

That's Iren's shadow. "The lovelorn girl from the long bridge fell," and her bones washed up on the Kneecap. You're holding one of them. She left her shadow behind, in this place, when she fell.

The shadow shouted back at them. *Iren wasn't lovelorn!*
No broken heart ever broke her head. There was fire. The house
burned. She jumped from a high window. She risked drowning
rather than let herself burn. She jumped, and she sang as she
jumped. She was a Fiddleway singer. She sang to bind her own
courage together, but the song broke mine. I was scared. I let her
voice cut us apart, so she fell without me. She drowned without
me. I stayed. I'm still here. I'm always here.

"I'm sorry," Kaile whispered. "I'm so sorry." She was
relieved to hear this version of the story. The flute and its
music had always felt stronger to her than a girl who died
of heartbreak.

You've brought a piece of her back, Iren's shadow whispered, sounding hopeful. *She's still trying to sing for the*
bridge.

We all have to hold the bridge together, Shade insisted,
or else there won't be a here for very much longer. Both of you
follow me.

Shade moved between charred and ruined pieces of
furniture, found a staircase, and began to climb by lantern
light.

Kaile hurried behind.

Iren's lost shadow came last.

They followed the sound of discord up to the very
highest room.

The ghoul crouched there beneath a shattered window frame.

It stood. It had grown huge and hulking since Kaile had seen it last. Rags of riverweed and rotting sails trailed behind it and caught in the glass shards of the ruined window.

It climbed up here, Kaile realized. *It's made of people who fell off the bridge—or who jumped off the bridge, or were pushed off the bridge—and now it's clawed its way back on.*

The ghoul filled the room with itself and its singing.

FIFTEENTH VERSE

THOUSANDS OF DROWNED BONES fit themselves together to form a single figure, using the song as both muscle and sinew. Claws of carved fishhooks made deep grooves in the wooden floor. Several skulls sat on its wide shoulders, each jaw open, each one singing.

The ghoul paid no mind to its new audience. It went on singing its own discordant version of the flood song. The sound scraped the ceiling and tumbled across the floor. It spread across the bridge to strike sideways at all other Fiddleway music.

There must be several former bridge musicians in there, Shade whispered. *They all know the song. They know how to sing it. They know how to twist it.*

"Why?" Kaile whispered back. "Why would it want to bring down the Fiddleway?"

Listen, Shade insisted. *There's pain and grief and despair and regret all jumbled into those notes, and now it wants to share that misery. It wants the rest of the bridge to drown with it, and feel all the pain that it can still remember feeling. Can't you hear it? Listen! The same music can bind or break. This song holds the ghoul together, and it will shake the bridge apart.*

Kaile heard it. She did not want to hear it, but she did. The sound of raw and open pain surrounded her.

Not her, the other shadow said. *Not Iren. She isn't in there. She never despaired.*

"We could try to drive it away again with 'The Counting Song,'" Kaile suggested, her voice very small. "One for the buns now overdone . . ." But this time it was the ghoul's voice that drove her own away. She faltered and fell silent.

That won't be enough, Shade whispered.

"Guess not," Kaile whispered back.

She looked at the flute in her hand. *You jumped from here,* she thought. *Maybe you jumped from this room and this window. But it wasn't for grief and heartbreak. You made a choice, a horrible choice. Stay and burn, or jump and probably drown—but maybe not. Maybe live. I'm sorry that you didn't.*

The ghoulish thing raised its arms, and it raised up the agony and violence of its voice. Robes of cloth and weeds billowed around and behind it as though underwater and moved by rough currents. Kaile cowered at the sound and shape of it.

"I can't fight that," she told Shade, her own voice hushed and hardly there.

You don't have to, Shade told her. *Redirect it. Guide it sideways. Make it a part of everything else.*

Kaile took up the flute and played.

It was the same song, always the same song. She played a duet with the ghoul, and tried to make the music match all the sounds that bridge and River made.

Not enough, Shade whispered. *Still not enough. Bind or break. Bind us together, or break the whole bridge down.*

Kaile felt a shiver. It traveled up from her feet to the tips of her hair.

She poured more of herself and her breath into the music.

She heard the fluid strength of floodwaters roaring, and that became part of the song.

She heard the bridge shift the weight of its stones, and that became part of the song.

She heard strains of music from each and every musician on the Fiddleway, passed through the air and between shadows. She heard Iren's lost shadow singing nearby. Kaile played alongside all of them.

Separate threads of sound braided together. The River and the city and the bridge in between, the drums and the strings and the voices and the footfalls all became one song—and that song swelled to include the ghoul.

Kaile held the bridge together. The dead thing fell apart.

It screamed, shrieked, and collapsed as thousands of separate bones fell. Skulls and ribs, combs and dice, fishhooks and finger bones clattered at Kaile's feet and were finally still.

✳ ✳ ✳

Kaile kept playing. The song held for as long as the flood lasted—which wasn't very long. The River's force ebbed, slowed, and finally passed downstream. The danger faded. The bridge stood.

She lowered her flute. Then she raised it again and tried the first few notes of "The Counting Song." The flute played it willingly, no longer bound to a single piece of music.

"Oh good," Kaile said, relieved. "I was hoping you'd let me play something else."

She looked for the shadows, and saw neither one of them. The lantern had already burned out. The only light streamed in through the broken window.

"Shade?" Kaile asked the empty room.

She heard nothing. A long and silent moment passed before Shade whispered back.

I'm here.

"Where?" Kaile asked. "I can't see you. And where is Iren's shadow?"

Gone, said Shade. The word sounded like a closed door, or the closing note of a song. It sounded like good-bye. Kaile didn't ask where the lost shadow had gone.

"I still can't see you," she said, looking around.

You have to let me lead sometimes, Shade told her.

Kaile remembered the shiver in her feet, just before the music wove itself together into one solid thing, and she began to understand.

"I will," she said. Her voice caught in her throat and stumbled a little.

You have to listen, Shade whispered.

"I know."

And try not to drag me through oily puddles in the road, or over dung piles.

"I'll try. I will. I promise."

Good.

Kaile stepped away from the fallen bones. She saw her shadow stretched out across the floor, moving when she moved, tied to her own two feet.

"Thank you," she said. She tucked lantern and flute into her satchel, and went downstairs.

✳ ✳ ✳

All of the Fiddleway music-makers stood outside the wreck of a house, waiting for Kaile.

Luce stood with them, leaning casually against a lamp-post and grinning wide.

Master Nibbledy stepped forward. He took Kaile's hand in both of his own.

"Musician," he said in his high, solemn voice.

SIXTEENTH VERSE

KAILE RODE A SOUTHSIDE carriage to Broken Wall in the early evening, pushed along by no one she knew. Luce Strumgut rode beside her. Bombasta the singer had a carriage all to herself, and sat upright and regal as though she rode in an actual carriage instead of a repurposed wheelbarrow.

"We could have just walked," Kaile said. She was nervous, doubtful, and in no hurry to actually arrive.

"Her ladyship the singer would not have walked," said Luce, waving one hand at Bombasta's carriage. "Bad for the vocal cords, or some such thing."

"Did she have to come with us?" Kaile asked. "Does it have to be her?"

"Yes," said Luce. "It does. This is her way of apologizing to you, and to me. If you don't let her apologize, then her disgruntlement will grow and she'll hate you forever. She might hate you forever anyway, of course, and for no reason in particular—but she is also our very best singer. You'll want to have our best singer for this, to make sure that it sticks."

"I suppose," said Kaile.

This is going to work, Shade whispered in her ear. *This is going to stick.*

Kaile wasn't nearly so sure. Her hand touched her shadow's hand where it rested on the bench.

She looked around to see several familiar places: Miss Mullusk's house, and Doctor Boggs's office clinic on Borrow Street, and the little lump of ground that everyone still called Watchtower Hill—even though it wasn't much of a hill, and no towers had actually stood on it for longer than anyone remembered. She watched the winding, dusty roadways of Southside as the wheelbarrows drew closer to Broken Wall.

Luce and Bombasta intended to perform a nameday song—the sort of song that tells newborn infants their names, and also tells the world.

"Do we have to do this tonight?" Kaile asked.

Luce looked down at her with a rough sort of sympathy. "It doesn't *have* to be tonight," the sailor said. "We could wait until tomorrow. We could wait until your old nameday, so the new one would match."

Kaile shook her head. "My old nameday is months from

now. I don't want to wait that long. I should just insist on getting presents both days—the old one and the new one."

The sailor grinned. "That's a fine plan, that is."

Kaile tried to smile. She almost managed. Then she gave up.

"I don't really think this is going to work," she admitted. "My family sang my funeral. The funeral's already over and sung. There's no taking that back—so they won't ever take me back."

"Wrong," said the sailor. "One ceremony trumps another. A divorce trumps a misguided wedding. A second bottle of fizzy wine smashed against the prow of a barge can rename it if the old name proved to be unlucky. We could even give *you* a new name tonight, if you like."

"No," said Kaile. "I like my name. And I'm not a barge."

"True enough," said Luce. "You aren't a barge. But you *are* getting a new nameday."

The wheelbarrow went over a bump in the road. The sailor cursed. Kaile just tried to hold on.

She still didn't know what had happened to the Baker's Cage. Maybe it had remained suspended above the rising waters. The flood had subsided quickly, and it hadn't climbed nearly so high as everyone had feared. Maybe Mother had been fine inside the cage. Or maybe it had toppled over and sunk to the very bottom of the River, drowning Mother inside it. Kaile still didn't know. Her thoughts burned with not knowing. But she was also afraid to finally find out.

The wheelbarrows stopped beside the alehouse.

Kaile didn't move. She didn't want to go in. If she went inside, then she might interrupt Mother's own funeral song.

Luce jumped down and hoisted her lute case. Shells woven into her braids clinked together. "Come on, girl," she said. "We have a gig to play."

This will work, Shade whispered again.

Kaile took a breath, and then another one. She climbed down from the wheelbarrow, her movements matched by her shadow.

* * *

The public room was full of patrons. Dozens of faces turned to look at them as they stood in the doorway.

Kaile noticed only one.

Mother's hair was still a mess. Her eyes looked shadowed and swollen, and she had ash stains rubbed over her cheekbones to show that she was in mourning—but she stood tall behind the counter, commanding the room. This place was a barge, and she the skipper of it, competent above all other things.

Mother wasn't drowned. She wasn't dead.

"I had to stay in the cage for hours longer than I was

supposed to, dangling over the washed-out docks," she told the customers up at the counter. "I don't suppose I'll have to go back tomorrow, though, and that's a small blessing."

Then she saw Kaile in the doorway. Her swollen eyes grew wide. She looked away. She looked down at the counter. She would not look at her daughter. Kaile's heart sank and drifted downstream.

Voices began whispering.

"Don't look."

"Don't catch her attention."

"Don't encourage her haunting."

"This is what comes of feeding a dead girl. They come back inside when they shouldn't ever, and they don't fade away when they should."

"Why don't they put louder charms over the threshold?"

"Don't look."

"Don't anybody look at her."

Kaile became the center of an empty space, a hole in the room that everyone ignored—everyone except the Snotfish, who stared at her from underneath a table.

He waved. Kaile waved back.

"She's got a shadow," the Snotfish pointed out. "She's got her shadow back."

People began to steal sideways looks at Kaile, and the floor at her feet.

Luce opened her lute case and tuned up her instrument. Bombasta cleared her throat with a scornful sound.

"This is Kaile's nameday," the singer announced, and made it true by saying it aloud.

She sang. Luce played. The music had much the same shape and movement as a funerary song, but used here to say hello rather than good-bye.

Other voices started to pick up the song. Other patrons joined in. The four domini players sang with reedy voices. The Snotfish sang, loud and out of tune. Father stood in the kitchen doorway and sang.

Mother looked up from behind the counter. She looked at Kaile. She looked directly at Kaile with guarded hope. She let her own voice join the music—even though she almost never sang anything.

Everyone in the room gave voice to a song of hello and of welcoming home.

Kaile stood with her shadow and listened.

ACKNOWLEDGMENTS

Thanks to my childhood music teachers, for their patience (I wasn't much of a musician). Thanks to Ivan, Nathan, Melon, and Jon, for their great love of song and karaoke. Thanks to my writing group, Symbolical Head, for their surgical workshopping skills; to Joe and Barry, for all their advice; and to Karen and Emily, for their editorial wisdom. Thanks to Zoe Keating, for the music I used as my writing soundtrack.